International P[illegible]

Stevie Smith, the brilliant and [illegible] *ist, has been widely praised for her contributions to the world of literature. Her insightful social observations have inspired many admirers. The author of nine books of poetry and three novels before her death in 1971, Stevie Smith has swiftly transcended her reputation as a classic contemporary English writer and has developed a far-reaching audience on an international scale. "Stevie," a moving and brilliant film, produced and directed by Robert Enders, and starring Glenda Jackson and Mona Washbourne, has garnered critical praise and received coveted awards from The New York Film Critics and the National Board of Review. Stevie Smith has now become an international sensation—a monument to the human spirit.*

"This novel has all of Stevie Smith's characteristics: odd and vivid perceptions, emotional candor and a delicate ruthlessness."

—*The Times*

"This famous novel still has the power to move the reader to laughter and tears."

—*The Manchester Evening News*

"Haunting . . . extraordinary handling of conversation . . . fascinating and recounted with a perfect ear . . ."

—*The Guardian*

"Recommended . . . inimitable . . ."

—*Good Housekeeping*

"Language that is deep and strong, changeable and moving."

—*The Sunday Telegraph Magazine*

"Gentle . . . elusive . . . surprising."

—*Punch*

"Remarkable."

—*Soho News*

Other Novels by Stevie Smith

THE HOLIDAY
OVER THE FRONTIER

Novel on Yellow Paper

a novel

by Stevie Smith

Introduction by Janet Watts

Preface by Mary Gordon

PINNACLE BOOKS  NEW YORK

This is a work of fiction. All the characters and events portrayed in this book are fictional, and any resemblance to real people or incidents is purely coincidental.

NOVEL ON YELLOW PAPER

A Pinnacle Book published by arrangement with Virago Ltd.

First printing, November 1982

ISBN: 0-523-41683-0

Printed in the United States of America

PINNACLE BOOKS, INC.
1430 Broadway
New York, New York 10018

NOVEL ON YELLOW PAPER

PREFACE

by Mary Gordon

Like all genuine eccentrics Stevie Smith believed herself supremely ordinary. The setting of her life was willed, stubbornly, rebelliously: a choice of genius in the comic mode, of camouflage and self-protection. She lived in the suburbs with her aunt. There was much in her of the hearty, slightly hysterical spinster: sherry at four, hot drinks at ten, and witty drawings hidden underneath the blotter of the sitting room desk. Every word she wrote balanced between terror and hilarity. No writer is more death struck, and no modern has her knack of finding in the detritus of ordinary life such cause for mirth.

Novel on Yellow Paper shares the preoccupations of all of Stevie Smith: laughter, literature, death. It is a novel of nerves: it jumps, darts, turns, shrieks with laughter, recoils in horror, runs for a book, settles down to weep in quiet at the great blank cruelty of human life. It is the story of Pompey Casmilus, a young woman who lives in the suburbs and works as a secretary for a kindly publisher of women's magazines. Pompey's vision is unfixed and always shifting. Death, madness, grief, peer over one shoulder, but behind the other is a sight so risible, a conversation so irresistable in its absurdity that death and madness, cruelty and grief must flee. At the end of the novel, Pompey is mourning her lost lover. She has decided that she is not right for marriage; that her rhythm is friendship with its comings and goings; that her beloved Freddy in his resolute small mindedness would choke her quite to death.

> And I was lying in bed, crying with influenza and exasperation when into my bedroom came my Aunt the Lion of Hull. There was going to be a church bazaar. Auntie Lion was going to the bazaar dressed as a fan. Now all the ladies of the parish were going to the bazaar as a fan. But Auntie Lion was not at one with her fan. Standing in front of the double mirror in the bedroom she was making lioning faces and noises because of the obstinacy of the fan: Now it is fixed how do I look?

But the genius of Stevie Smith is not a serene one: it does not bring about resolutions, moments of stasis. No sooner has she enjoyed the sight of her aunt dressed as a fan, than she is overcome with love for her, and fears her loss. And, within a page, she tells us of her mother's painful death,

> What can you do? You can do nothing but be there, and go on being there steadily and without a break until the end. There is nothing but that that you can do. My mother was dying, she had heart disease, she could not breathe, already there were the cylinders of oxygen. There was the nurse and the doctor coming day and night. But if you cannot breathe how can you breathe the oxygen? Even, how can the doctors help you. Or? You must suffer and then you must die. And for a week this last suffering leading to death continued. Oh how much better to die quickly. Oh then afterwards they say: Your mother died quickly. She did not suffer. You must remember to be thankful for that. But all the time you are remembering that she did suffer. Because if you cannot breathe you must suffer. And the last minute when you are dying, that may be a very long time indeed. But of course the doctors and the nurses have their feet very firmly upon the ground, and a minute to them is just sixty seconds' worth of distance run. So now it is all over, it is all over and she is dead. Yes, it is all over it is all over it is.

What a great deal of life we are taken over in three pages. The loss of young love, the hilarity of suburban manners, filial devotion, and suffering, the coldness of the objective vision, the finality of death. The comprehensiveness, the range, of this short passage, its sheer interest, its felicity—all are possible only because the narrative voice is finely and deliberately controlled at every moment. The seemingly throwaway "*well*" 's, "*and*" 's, "*now*" 's, the parody diminutives, the quick, short repetitions, are anything but throwaway in fact. They create the illusion of the spoken voice; they capture the nervous aural genius of the brilliant talker. It is a voice determined to take itself unseriously, yet to speak of all that is most serious in life. It is a social voice, a party voice. Above all, it wishes not to bore; above all, it wishes to be amusing. For the speaker, Pompey, cannot keep out of her mind—even as she tells us about funny clippings she has cut from the Women's Pages—visions of horror, of cruelty that have struck her with the terrors of the damned in hell.

She tells us she has seen the devil. Not for her the almost comforting fiend with its iconographic wings, tail, leer. Not, she tells us,

> . . . anything at all of the dark mind of Milton soaring up over the dark abyss, very damned and noble. No this was the fiend that is neither like Goethe's Mephistophles, that almost too impudent spirit of negation.

She sees the devil on the streets of Hythe after she is recovering from the flu.

> . . . up on the hills by the canal, there were pieces of paper, and there were cartons that had held ice cream and there were those little cardboard spoons that go with it. And there were newspapers and wrapping papers.
>
> There was every sort of paper there, only the devil was there too, and he was not wrapped up in paper.
>
> It was a dreadful vision that I had there of the heart of this fiend. And every stormisch and sad I was too, and full of the black night of foreboding, and when I came back to the hotel I was very profoundly disturbed. Very horrified and bristling with the breath of the frightful fiend was Pompey.

The vision, it its very formlessness, its emptiness, its ordinariness, is the true heart of darkness. Papers on the street in a holiday town: the devil. The horror is real. And yet, Pompey's diction tries to make light of her horror; the jump into self-parody, the use of the swallowed whole German "Stormisch", the children's book inversion "very terrified and bristling with the breath of the frightful fiend was Pompey." Yet the horror remains. Yet it does not remain forever. There is so much to talk about. There is the list of funny quotations to bring out. We must be told the story of *Phedre*, of the *Bacchae*. There are wonderful friends me must meet. And the important decision must be discussed: will she marry Freddy?

The pace of *Novel on Yellow Paper* is slightly frantic; it is marked, almost, by a determination never to be still. For stillness might reveal the truth that Pompey fears above all else, the vision she gets glimpses of: there may be nothing at the center, things may not be what they seem. She had her first glimpse of this possibility as a child, in a tuberculosis sanitorium when a nurse maid takes her on her knee.

> If I was in the mood for it I could play up to her fancy, but even while I was doing this I was immensely terrified. Her feeling for me, I felt this very keenly but could not for some time understand why it so much dismayed me, was in outward appearance, so far as being hugged and set on her knee, was what in outward appearance my mother . . . ? No, do you see, but it was profoundly disturbing, how in essence her feeling was so arbitrary, so superficial, so fortuitous. And so this feeling she had for me, which was not at all a deep feeling, but as one might pet, pat and cuddle a puppy, filled me with the fear that a child has in the face of cruelty. It was so insecure, so without depth or significance. It was so similar in outward form, and so asunder and apart, so deceitful and so barbarous in significance. It very profoundly disturbed and dismayed and terrified me.

It is then, as a child, that she learns to think of death as a friend, to reckon suicide a blessing and a comfort.

The voice we hear throughout the novel is a voice whose function is to cover over terror. Pompey is forever terrified; she feels at every moment her utter vulnerability, as if she were a burn victim, unhealed. She loves Racine, the Greeks, because they present the possibility of imperviousness. One is struck, time and again, by the central moral virtue in all of Stevie Smith's work: courage. For it is an act of the highest morality to swallow terror whole, to allow oneself to be distracted by the Lion Aunt, the advice in the Lovelorn Column, the fate of Phedre and Pnetheus on the mountain. Pompey is self absorbed, but she is not a narcissist. Against tremendous odds, she goes on loving life.

And so, *Novel on Yellow Paper* is a tale of heroism comically told, a heroism deeply modern: the triumph over the terror of the human condition. Stevie Smith has much in common, after all, with Kafka: the horror of the meaningless, the obsession with the ordinary details and routine of modern life. But where he falls into despair, she ends up laughing. The final vision of *Novel on Yellow Paper* is, to be sure, a vision of death. But it is the death of the tigress Flo, affronted by the insult of having been offered artificial respiration by the zookeeper.

> She looked, she lurched, and seeing some last, unnameable, not wholly apprehended final outrage, she fell, she whimpered, clawed in vain, and died.

But Pompey the tigress lives on. She cannot die just yet; she has much more to tell us.

INTRODUCTION

Stevie Smith first tried to get her poems published in 1935, but was told by a publisher to 'go away and write a novel'. The same publisher was foolish enough to turn down the result of his advice, *Novel on Yellow Paper*, as too much of a risk; but when Jonathan Cape brought it out in 1936 it won for its author a *succès fou* and instant celebrity. 'A work of genius', in the influential opinion of Naomi Mitchison; 'a curious, amusing, provocative and very serious piece of work', pronounced *The Times Literary Supplement*.

Some decades later, Stevie Smith expressed to her friend Kay Dick a rather dimmer personal view of the work that was to be succeeded by two more novels and several volumes of poetry. She had written it under the influence of Dorothy Parker, whom she had been reading just before writing it, she said, and now found a lot of things in it dated, mannered, and 'brassy'.

Such self-depreciation was characteristic of Stevie Smith, both as a woman and a writer, but within *Novel on Yellow Paper* itself it overlays an equally typical *insouciance* and perceptible pride. On an early page she warns the foot-on-the-ground person that it was a mistake ever to buy this book: for him it will be a desert of weariness and exasperation. 'for this book is the talking voice that runs on', and the voice belongs to Pompey Casmilus, a person whose feet are well off the ground. Useless to her, the good advice of people to write 'the sort of book the plain man in the street will read. . . . Because I can write only as I can write only, and Does the road wind uphill all the way? Yes, to the very end. But brace up, chaps, there's a 60,000 word limit.'

As an apology, it is graceful, but scarcely grovelling; and it has to stretch a good way to cover a book that rivals *Tristram Shandy* in doing so shamelessly just what its author pleases. The talking voice of Pompey Casmilus flirts and fools with its reader and subject-matter alike. It stops and starts, it dodges and teases. It picks up a person or an idea and drops them flat out of sudden boredom; it plays with words and speech-patterns. It speaks different languages, puts on foreign accents and funny disguises; it quotes from the literature of remote countries and centuries and the trash of contemporary England.

It is its mistress's voice indeed: a delicate and extraordinary instrument. Stevie Smith's friends remember her talk with love, and the strange unity of her character and her writing. 'The poetry wasn't so much a projection of her personality, as an integral part of it. It was her voice itself,' Norah Smallwood recalls. 'Her quality was one of her poems. If you'd known Stevie you'd hardly have needed her poetry, because knowing Stevie was enough,' in the memory of Marghanita Laski.

And yet—as the author apostrophises in her book—'Oh talking voice that is so sweet, how hold you alive in captivity, how point you with commas, semi-colons, dashes, pauses and paragraphs?' She does it, as we might expect, with enjoyment and *elan*. 'The thoughts come and go and sometimes they do not quite come and I do not pursue them to embarrass them with formality to pursue them into a harsh captivity . . .'

The thoughts come: she does not pursue them. Stevie Smith had that kind of mind, a consciousness on which, it would seem, a multitude of realities wrote themselves, whether she wanted them to or not. She led an apparently quiet and uneventful life, a spinster living in Palmers Green with her aged aunt: yet she neither missed nor escaped anything that was going on in the world outside her own. Everything touched her, and in this book she thinks about everything. She thinks about fear, love, death, marriage, celibacy and sex. She thinks about religion, boredom, suicide, abortion and bliss.

In this is the surprising universality of this most individual of writers. Stevie-Pompey thinks and talks and writes about her own (usually very quirky) experience, and speaks for us all. Through Pompey Casmilus, elated to be the only goy at an all-Jewish party, or wretched at the covert brutality in contemporary Germany, we may realize and recognize what anti-semitism is. Through her laughable and sad *affaires* we may share her perceptions of love and friendship, of English suburbia, of the Chekhovian dreams of young women, of social and intellectual snobbery, of human suffering.

The thoughts come: 'and the people come too, and come and go, to illustrate the thoughts, to point the moral, to adorn the tale'. The novel is full of people. 'All my friends, my beautiful and lovely friends' are bidden goodbye in its first paragraph, for a reason not difficult for the reader to work out for himself. The talking voice is accompanied by an eye whose humour and warmth do not veil its merciless clarity. They turned the baby Pompey to face the other way in her pram. 'With Stevie for a friend, one didn't need enemies,' one of her closest circle told me.

Friends, acquaintances, enemies; figures from history and ancient myth; characters created by beloved writers; the *dramatis personae* of the gossip of friends—all are people for Pompey's thoughts. We glimpse them as they come and go in her talk: spotlit for a moment in the dazzlingly sharp focus of her perceptions, to be banished as swiftly as the movement of her mind. Chic Leonie rides with a poor kneegrip in Rotten Row; Freddy holds Pompey close in a country churchyard in late-afternoon rain. Dionysius laughs in the valley as Pentheus toils uphill to his death; Cynthia, who lived free, trails a social-worker's horde of brattos around London. A trainload of British sit in frozen hatred of the invader of the seat marked Reserved; Pompey weeping for the evils of Nazism is saved by the sly filch of a fellow-traveller's *Lady Chatterley's Lover*.

The people come and go, vividly and robustly alive in their moment, between their entrances and exits, but born and dead at the dictates of their creator's reflections, memories and whims. All but one. One person does not come and go in this most personal of novels. At every moment—even through the long quotations, the résumés of favourite books—we hear the voice of Pompey Casmilus; and no character in her book's vivid company is more sharply and tellingly revealed than her own. Like many first novels, *Novel on Yellow Paper* tells the story of its writer's life, and the throwaway wit does not conceal its stark lines. It was a life blighted by the ill health of Stevie Smith's childhood, the death of her mother and the desertion of her father.

It was also a life filled with friendship and love. The friends are here, and some of the lovers. The book crackles with Pompey's crisp parcelling-up of Karl, and shimmers with the swaying of her feelings for Freddy. Curiously, it is in this area most difficult to talk about that Pompey's voice becomes most eloquent:

> And between two people without knowing it a love may grow up, and a link may form, and no one knows or guesses. And so it has been. I did not know. But when it is over, it is over, then it is tearing inside, it is 'tearing in the belly', one would wish oneself dead and unborn. And one does little things and goes to see friends and does one's work and fusses with this and that and feels in one's heart the drift and dribble of penultimate things, and thinks: Tomorrow I shall be dead.

Stevie Smith defied suburbia and all its tennis clubs; braved loneliness and old maidhood; foreswore marriage. She was tigerishly proud of the powerful feelings behind her spinster exterior, and shortly before her death she told a friend to correct people's belief that 'because I never married I know nothing about the emotions. When I am dead you must put them right. I loved my aunt.' The redoubtable old lady who nurtured Stevie Smith from babyhood, and was cared for by her in turn until she died, was the constant, profound, irradiating love of Stevie Smith's life. No portrait in this book is more affectionately drawn, more tenderly apologized for.

Janet Watts, 1980

Casmilus, whose great name I steal,
Whose name a greater doth conceal,
Indulgence, pray,
And, if I may,
The winged tuft from either heel.

Beginning this book (not as they say 'book' in our trade—they mean magazine), beginning this book, I should like if I may, I should like, if I may (that is the way Sir Phoebus writes), I should like then to say: Good-bye to all my friends, my beautiful and lovely friends.

And for why?

Read on, Reader, read on and work it out for yourself.

Here am I on a fine day in October riding along the Row with Leonie. Well, please do not think that I have a lot of money. But here I am all the same. And who is paying? Well, partly it is like this. You see, they run cheap rides in the Row. On cheap horses? Well no, not that either so much. Well, here goes my horse. He is better than that horse I had this year in Cornwall, that horse that was called Kismet. He was a great eater, was Kismet. No sooner pause than crop the verdure. He had a scythelike movement of his long head, of his long snakelike neck. Oh ho Kismet. He could crop a wall of its plant life soon as any horse I have ever seen. He was the great Horse that laid waste the Duchy of Cornwall. You should have seen Kismet get down to the growing corn. It grew no more after that this year. Well, Kismet, I hope the farmers looked at it that way, see?

But this horse I am on now, with Leonie looking chic and capable beside me, this horse is a good horse. He puts his ears back and dances sideways across the shadows. It is a hot sunny day and does not seem as if November was coming soon. It is a hot sunny day but the earth smells like it had a layer of frost on top, and the leaves are brittle and whisk up and under your nose and across the earth beds. That is how it is in October. I look at Leonie, she has very good hands but her kneegrip is not so-o-o good. Leonie is a Jewess, but slim, and has a sense of *chic*. She is looking very elegant. She has a yellow pullover and fawn jodhpurs and a fawn felt hat. And who cares.

Last week I was at a party at Leonie's. Suddenly I looked round. I thought: I am the only goy. There was a newspaper man there and a musician and some plain business men. But the Jews. Well all to say about the Jews has been said, so I'll leave it. But then I had a moment of elation at that party. I got shot right up. Hurrah to be a goy! A clever goy is cleverer than a clever Jew. And I am a clever goy that knows everything on earth and in heaven. This moment of elation I am telling you about: the only living person in that room, the cleverest person in that room; the cleverest living goy.

Do all goys among Jews get that way? Yes, perhaps. And the feeling you must pipe down and apologize for being so superior and clever: I can't help it really my dear chap, you see I'm a goy. It just comes with the birth. It's a world of unequal chances, not the way B. Franklin saw things. But perhaps he was piping down in public, and apologizing he was a goy. And there were Jews then too. So he put equality on paper and hoped it would do, and hoped nobody would take it seriously. And nobody did.

Oh how lovely this is all now in London in October. And how lovely to be living, a goy and a Londoner. I have a lot of Jewish friends. It makes me feel januslike, doublefaced. Nobody knows but me what I think about that thing. But I get behaving as if they did know, and I had to pipe down and apologize, and not seem to be taking credit for the happy accident of Nordic birth. There is nothing so superior as that false humility, and nothing that has made so much trouble, and nothing that will go on making trouble so long as things are. Oh quiet, now, quiet. Didn't I say all to say had been said?

The thought that comes to me now, that I am riding this horse, that puts his ears back and dances across the shadows, and glances with hatred and panic at the white gate posts, is the thought of all that I wish to say in this book, is the thought that works at me like a worm, like an intestinal worm that pulls and drags its alexandrine length along those five hundred yards of trouble. *Mrs. Haliburton's Troubles,* that is a book I read when I was a young child. Sometimes I think I have read too much. There were those titles of books I used to read-ride-ahobby-horse. Riding crops up and crops take me right back to Kismet. Hobby-horse whoa-up. That book *Mrs. Haliburton's Troubles*. Not a thing can I remember about that book except that Mrs. Haliburton—or perhaps there were two ells—had troubles enough which she bore up under and preserved a stiff upper lip, smiling to the end, when God stepped in and made all right.

There was then another title that I remember with humble thankfulness, also a minor Victorian, here it is then: *Lost Sir Massingberd,* called by the clever boys of those days: 'Lost Sir Missing-Bird'. Well, do it better yourself. This was a baronet that got trapped up in a hollow oak on his landed estates and there he died. And if you read this book you see how Providence tidies things up, yes, and keeps the right people the right side of calamity, and the oak tree gets the delinquent. Providence does that in books of that period, which I read as a young child sitting in my paternal grandfather's library at Scaithness, Lincs.

How richly compostly loamishly sad were those Victorian days, with a sadness not nerve-irritating like we have to-day. How I love those damp Victorian troubles. The woods decay, the woods decay and fall, The vapours weep their burthen to the ground, Man comes and tills the field and lies beneath, And after many a summer dies the swan. Yes, always someone dies, someone weeps, in tune with the laurels dripping, and the tap dripping, and the spout dripping into the water-butt, and the dim gas flickering greenly in the damp conservatory.

And the laurels so teeming and close along the drive, a human foot was bound to feel there was something behind it all. *Behind the laurel bushes lay the corpse of Sir Vyvyan Markaby, Baronet.*

Then I think of the wild wet days of the wild wet Lincolnshire of the younger Tennyson. How, were there two? Yes, but I mean younger than the pet of the Old Queen. Younger and sadder. Oh the sad sweet over-sweet Alfred, so haughty, so proud and so disagreeable.

And thinking of all this I have a great *nostalgie* for an open drain, like the flooded dykes they have there between the sodden fields. Like that picture when I was a child. We always went for the summer to some little cottage by the sea where they left the furniture and the pictures behind and the coarse clean linen sheets. And the smell of country stuffy rooms. And there on the wall was this picture. It turned up like the finger of God. In Lincs, where we were at Saltfleet. In Norfolk where we were at Heacham. In Suffolk too, if my countries are right, where we were at Pakefield, there was that picture.

There is a vast flooded prairie, a rushing mud-yellow foam-curded rain-lashed torrent, as if all the dams in the world were burst; swirling pushing leaping around, not hardly Christian, not Christian at all, but just the old element at its savagery, and no different from what it was before Anno Domini came that should daunt the flood. And riding—hick horse well met Kismet, whoa up, I say, whoa up—riding, now take it easy, on top of that brown flood was A little child shall ride it, in a cradle with a cat on top. Well I never, look at that thar cat, never mind the b-a-b-y, ain't that cat cunning? And all around engulfing desolation and a dark sky sending down rain so solid you could eat it. That baby in that cradle on that yellow brown sweeping flood makes me feel homesick now.

These childhood impressions make a difference, as the psycho-analysts charge a pound an hour for saying. Not that I've a word against the analysts, they make their living and when I think of what one woman must have suffered from Bennie saying all that was in his mind he could lay his hand to for one solid hour every day, and Sundays only off, I think that one pound a time is earned. I'll tell you about Bennie? Of course I'll tell you about Bennie, and about all my friends. You look back and see what I say at the beginning of this book.

I am typing this book on yellow paper. It is very yellow paper, and it is this very yellow paper because often sometimes I am typing it in my room at my office, and the paper I use for Sir Phoebus's letters is blue paper with his name across the corner 'Sir Phoebus Ullwater, Bt.' and those letters of Sir Phoebus's go out to all over the world. And that is why I type yellow, typing for my own pleasure, and not sending it by clerical error to the stockbrokers for a couple of thou. in Tekka Taiping, and not sending it to the Chief of Police with a formal complaint, and not sending it to Great Aunt Agatha asking her to, and asking her to . . .

Well look this dangerous way I am running on. I am a private secretary. And how is Sir

Phoebus? And how is his . . . ? and how is . . . ? I regret I am not in a position to state. No, that grand remark I am never able to make, and partly I think it is because it is often being too much of the truth. I am afraid I am not in a position to state. And I am afraid I should be. And I feel a desperate character. And then I think of a lot of hurrying jobs to do. There is the job-job-job of tearing up old letters. But that involves black face Phoebus, and darling Sir Baronet he gets bored quickly like me by fool unnecessary jobs that are not at all asking to be done.

And I will say this, and hang the consequences, Herbert, the great link between us two is the happy way we both get quickly bored. And do I worry him with fool unnecessary queries? I do not. We indulge in the utmost limit of boredom, he in his room and I in mine, and stagger out when tea time comes, as it must, however it comes, whether rung for on the house phone, or trundled in by the hired girl, that's like an angel of grace breaking in on the orgy of boredom to which my soul is committed.

It needs a good woman, or a good girl will do, to bring you back from the stony desert that runs up flat to a precipice where the soul hangs by a thread over the abyss. And what is down below? Hell. And don't say you don't believe in hell or hell may get the laugh of you. And hanging by a sisal twist over the darkling void lit by an electric blue flash, like mending the tram lines, you know that blue flash?—that's where the souls of smarties go, and that's where they hang over till tea time comes, and the bright happy smiling face of the young girl that's never been those places but just takes things as she finds them, not meaning loose change.

When I think what my work is, I think God has been very good to me. Like that drawing I saw today in an American paper. It made me laugh. There was the Naughty standing in a mink coat, and the sugar dad was there with the cheque-book sitting alongside, and all give-lovey looking. And there's Naughty saying just what I said, only not honest to God as I mean.

There's no sugar dad in my life and those looking for sugar dads can shut up here and throw back at Miss-in-Boots cash chemists book-store.

Sir Phoebus gets bored quickly. That's something to be glad about. The staying power of many magnates is surprising. You'd wonder they could do so many things like statistics and graphs and know-all-nothings. There's that Sir 'I Name no Names' who never writes a letter under seven pages close typescript. And does he get bored? No. But three secretaries he's worn down since last autumn, and didn't I say it is now October?

This Sir Nameless has a low church religious revival breath about him like a coffin. Everyone's a brother to him, 'all Cains and

Abels' that Sir Cale Spring Rice said I believe, the boy that was at the British Embassy, not the poet whose name I've got mixed in. That's the way Sir Nameless makes his money. And does. And does oh.

I do so hope Sir P. makes a lot of money. Oh I do so hope he does. I can't wish him better than that, or more what he'd wish himself. And like him, I cannot help but like him.

The only way I can lose myself is by doing those cables. We have a secret code which I have simplified because as it was you can have too much of a good thing. There was too much fancy footwork in the old way code. So I simplified it, and now it is just a nice clean game to help you forget there's sixty seconds run off to every minute.

In the old days a double-barrelled five-letter code cable would take upwards of six hours to decode. And the boys at the other end weren't as bright at it as we were, and like as not the lazies would sit round waiting for the letter confirming to arrive, and not owning up they couldn't get the hang of it at all. Such is human pride, friend, no, Brother, such is human pride and frailty. So now we've got it all prinked up and tidied and a child could use it, Sir, yes, Sir, if it could count and had the code sheet by.

By and by I'm going to step further on the upward grade and going to invent a code that doesn't need a code sheet, but you do it in your head, standing on your head, with one hand tied behind, and altering the run of numerals according to the date, see? Simple? Of course it's simple.

I am a forward-looking girl and don't stay where I am. 'Left right, Be bright,' as I said in my poem. That's on days when I am one big bounce, and have to go careful then not to be a nuisance. But later I get back to my own philosophical outlook that keeps us all kissable. It isn't always a private secretary and a magnate that don't go making trouble for themselves that meet. But when they do it makes you feel there's something in creation for all the dirt the cynics say.

Now Reader, don't go making trouble fixing up names to all this. I say here there's not a person nor a thing in this book that ever stepped outside of this book. It's just all out of my head. And don't go looking like a sick cat for wicked envy, it's a thing you might come to yourself: if you'd got the sort of head I have. And don't get despairing either. Remember what they said in the thirteen hundreds: 'Accidie poisons the soul stream'.

But I am not one to carry my work around with me out of office hours. I am a very lucky girl and have a great many dear friends out of the office, as I was saying I'd tell you about later. What I admire most in my women friends is what I get in Harriet. She makes me laugh. Second, she has a great sense of *chic*. Third, she is lovely to stay with.

Did I tell you my name was Pompey Casmilus? Patience I was christened, but later on when I got grown up and out and about in London, I got called Pompey. And it suits me. There's something meretricious and decayed and I'll say, I dare say, elegant about Pompey. A broken Roman statue. One of those old Roman boys that lost their investments and went round getting free meals on their dear old friends, that had them round to fill up the gaps, and keep things moving.

I don't mind saying I am a lucky girl and get entertained pretty freely one way and another. And a lot of my friends, now it is funny how it has all turned out, have moved away to the country. So now I go weekending, and there you get new angles on life. And there's not one of them where I go that's not lovely to stay with, excepting some whom I won't put in just here to strike a minor key.

Things being as they are nowadays, naturally you cannot live on for ever like this. Though a few years back, well say after the war, there was Cyril the Sponge who was real cunning and made a whole time job of it. But then when you get that way you have no real freedom for soul communing as I do. Take this Cyril for instance. He was the cousin of a cousin of mine from the U.S.A. that married a girl, as she was then, in 1920, it may have been. Well this girl was christened Gladys, but of course that wouldn't do. So later on she got herself called Prunella, which is a whole lot better, though linking up, by the tyranny of the association of ideas, like I read in Max Nordau, with intestinal stasis. And what do you know about that, Mr. Arch-Enemy-of-Elimination-Celia-Celia-Celia-Swift?

Well then, this cousin of mine, who is Prunella's husband, made money. And the more he made, the more he made. And the more he made, the more Prunella tickled him up and tricked him out with all the right turns of speech. And he could go anywhere, and nobody noticed. And so could she. And nobody did. They were just splendid, thank you. And always they made more and more money, and they had two children, and Prunella saw that they got brought up with the right ideas from the beginning. And they did. *'My dear*, isn't he just like an English gent? You'd never know.' Nobody did. Nobody would. There's nobody *to* know. Who cares?

Prunella got the children right on to the right books. You know the stuff they slop out to the little B.B.C. brattery? So wide-eyed and daisy-sweet, and solemn-young and sweet sweet smell of childhood, as Medea said, the moment she jabbed the knife into the couple of them to spite Jason. But of course they were never married. *My dear*, that makes all the difference. Only an emotional careerist could have run off with a foreigner and—hang the wedding. And we all know what emotional careerists are like when there are knives left lying around.

But it is not necessary to dwell on these horrid, horrid things, when there is so much in life that is pie-eyed and daisy-sweet. Is it? Are there not?

About the time the children were six and four years old, Cyril fell:

> As falls the gravelled grouse
> From a clear sky,
> Or as the clear eyed hawk,
> Sighting through skyey spaces
> Some lesser creature, formed and nurtured
> By the dear gods for his peculiar pleasure,
> Down plunges through the empyrean blue
> And takes what is his own,
> What rightly,
> Time, place, circumstances harmonious,
> Does, with the ageing of a weary world,
> Escheat to him.

That bit, from 'fell', is a poem I wrote, the way I wrote that other one I was saying and never got published. That's two off my hands. Though that last bit is but an excerpt from an unfinished manuscript of twenty-six pages single-spaced typewriting, and now temporarily laid by until the time is ripe. Read that bit again and you've got Cyril, and the whole Cyril, and nothing but Cyril. Always of course *mutatis mutandis*—which is the reader's job anyway.

Cyril dropped in to stay with the family for a week-end. And on and off he was there until he died of syncope two years back. Is not that pretty good going, seeing that he'd never tried it on before, not on that cousin, anyway?

And how the idea came to him was seeing my cousin's name on a prospectus some half-wit dropped into his letter box one day. Ha ha, did Cyril *underwrite?* No, not he. He understudied. He understudied the Nanny, and the mother's help, and the cookie-darling. Such a character was cookie. A character like that old cookie, I remember her well, helps a lot to build up an old-established reputation for social rightness. And he understudied them very well. And he taught the children to play bridge, when Prunella and my cousin wanted a day off, and the Nanny was staying with her sick married sister, the way they do. And he looked well. I mean *handsome,* not just healthy. Though for that matter there was nothing wrong with Cyril's health, not to say a creak or a murmur, till he dropped dead on them of syncope, as I said. And he helped Pru with the gardening she did, having herself a great natural taste for it, that was at the same time so right in that country place they dwelt in.

And I remember staying weekends there too, only in an amateurish way, not to cut Cyril out, though he looked as if he thought it was. And I got the thought I'd have a look into this gardening. And so I asked Prunella the names of what she was planting up. And sure enough back it comes to me now as clear as ever: Anchusa. And do I remember it had blue flowers? I do. I'd know an anchusa anywhere. But you don't want to get stuck at one thing too long and I remember anchusa and let the rest go. But Cyril the Sponge he was thorough. He never did things by half: and look at him now, dead of syncope. A live Pompey is better then a dead Cyril. As I said to myself the other day: a live Pompey is better than a dead lord—looking at a portrait of the great dead newspaper proprietor, that sharp-witted peer with a flair for forensic penny-a-lining, that came into my life when I ws twenty-four, sitting in my room and writing this poem about Russia that is twenty-six pages long and more to come.

By and by I mean to publish these poems I am talking about in book form. But, Reader, any poem you may read in these pages you may take it from me has never yet been published: so you get the first look in.

Sir Phoebus is now away on holiday and has to-day sent me a large double-sized tin of Harrogate toffee. It is that sort of thing about Sir Phoebus that makes him stand out head and shoulders above the ordinary run of baronets. It is that something.

Stupid people now for instance do not care so-o-o very much for Sir Phoebus's mama, but I can't help remembering that when I was once doing some work for her, I remember now it was called Twenty Thousand Leagues, no, Miles, Up the Amazon, that I was writing for her, and she just left me free to draw on my imagination.

And was that difficult? No, it was not. Because when I was a young child at my kindergarten school my very first memories are bound up with the cunning way we used to construct out of cardboard dress-boxes, loaned from home, a tropical forest. We put the lid up vertical, and just went full steam ahead, sloshing at it with paints. My favourite I remember now was indigo. I liked the name of it and the colour looked fine, set off with bice-green. Well on the box-part put horizontal at the foot of the lid we got plants of moss and toadstool and mould. And a fine mess it was, the sort that would keep a child quiet and happy. And there was our tropical forest as simple and as life-like as you please.

And about in that thar forest there crawled and swung and flew monkeys and apes and parrots, and jaguars and panthers, and all our four footed friends. And not so dumb either. What with the growling and whining and hissing and clatter that went on, it might have been Piccadilly with the road up.

Our instructress, she had a real talent for making jungles come alive to a child of tender years. And later I remember now she quit teaching and went studying Egyptology with Flinders Petrie, that man who was at the Loan Exhibition the other day, wearing a pink tie.

So this is how I did not find it difficult to write up Sir Phoebus's ma's journey up the Amazon. Moreover I had the help of a Scot who had been consul in those parts. And I remember now he wrote page after page of close written what he called data, and hardly a word of it could I read. So I let it go.

I guess what was wanted was a human story and not wise-cracks about the habits of the natives, which would not come too well anyway from Sir Phoebus's ma.

And that's the sort of thing you have to be careful of, and it's thinking of that sort of thing makes me the good secretary I am and makes up for my not being able to type with more than one finger on each hand. And as I always say, you want to keep thinking of all the things a person can do and not go brooding over what might have been.

Every day I was up there at Mabel Lady U.'s house, sure enough at four o'clock up came the sort of tea that can be associated only with a woman of great heart and real refinement. There were sandwiches rolled up round the right sort of stuffing, and cakes and scones, besides the tea, that was what I like, namely Earl Grey's mixture. And the best thing the old boy ever did, not counting out the League of Nations, as Sir P. always says.

Don't you see what I mean about this family and about the way people are good to me, and how lucky I am? And often I think I have a sword hanging over my head that must fall one day, because I am conscious of sin in my black heart and I think that God is saving up something special that will carry Pompey away. Like that flood that kid rode in its cradle with that thar cunning cat sitting atop of it. And perhaps if the kid rode the flood o.k. that thar cat smothered it. For you can't escape your fate. And I've known cats overlay babies. It was in the newspapers.

Readers, do you ever feel sea-sad, loamishly-sad, like Tennyson, with that sadness too deep for words? Though of course nothing is too deep for words for a poet like him and me. I mean the deeper the better as they say *je grösser der Schmerz desto besser das Kind*.

I think of my poems as my kiddo, and no doubt but Tennyson felt that way too, 'Deep as first love and wild with all regret, Oh death in Life the days that are no more.' And another one I'm set on is that one about that sick lady: 'And like a dying lady lean and pale.'—Lean and pale, that's just how I am these sad November days. For it is now November as it was October when I wrote before. So I'm getting on and sticking to my typewriter, and come Christmas this book will be ready for binding in limp yap and setting on your rich aunt's breakfast plate next the crumpled corn.—That 'like a dying lady lean and pale', I now come to reflect, is not Tennyson but Shelley.

I enjoy these moments of sadness and relish them to the uttermost deep. And now I like to go walks alone, and I have a fine walk at home that is just the thing. You go along a river that is dug in deep like a canal, and there are weeds alongside it seeps up through. And near the bank there is bright, brown mud, lovely with pin holes in it, because I suppose the river rats have been at it. blowing through.

By and by this river that was deep and narrow opens up and gets wide and shallow, so the mud sticks up through at places, and there is curded yellow green bits of foam on it, and there is an island in the middle there, where the trees bend over and trail their branches as if they were so cosmically bored they could think of nothing but to trail their finger tips. Like some boating excursions I've been on.

By and by of course the seeping mud and those rat holes get into your soul and you get shot up again, elated as I was at that Jew party. And I always think those wet wild rain-swept days are the days I most like. Because a heat wave and all the fixed hard colours take it out of you, but these days of murk and mess and a high wind, if I can have that too, puts it back into you again. So that I am twice what I ever was before these days.

And once I remember when I was walking along with Karl near Hertford a wet day like this I am telling you about, there in the road was a dead vole sticking its paws upright—like a Christian it had been run over.

Karl was a fine boy and we got on fine. He only had two suits of clothes over here and he always thought of this when it came to getting through hedges, as it must. He had a bad way sometimes of getting cross and cantankerous as if he was on the defensive all the time. Do you know how it is with foreigners? They can't let alone but must for ever be telling you how they do things back home. Karl certainly was a sweet boy, bar this.

There's something of Mrs. Humphry Ward in me. I mean these damp fields and sad woods and queer looking Victorian castles with moss-grown paths. And I well remember going with Karl up the path like this to an empty house. There was a forlorn look about that house. There were bars on the windows and a half basement. You could guess the sordid lives of the domestic girl. Yes 'lives' I mean in the plural, that was no slip-up of the typewriter, for I guess she had to have a compensating night-life after the mutton fat and the cabbage-washing and dish-washing was done or piled up out of sight. And good luck to her. And I hope she never got caught, or appeared in trouble, for people didn't believe in sex those days like they do now.

But to get the peculiar flavour of those days and those ways of thinking you must read the novels of the period. It's no use to think you can get it by reading what's written nowadays all strung up and strung out and bad bottom false. Oh, how those books make me yawn, yes, and make me sad too, but not that loamish sadness the way I love.

When Karl and I got up to that house, it stood back in the wood, it began to rain with the utmost abandon of despair. So thinking of his two suits of clothes, and myself wanting to get into the house, I did, through a broken window at the back. May I say now that I am slim and agile, and that pantry window wasn't the first by a long cheese I had got in at.

Karl too was a good climber, but being six feet two inches, though not plump, he had to look around and find another broken window more his size. Well, as all the windows were broken that was not hard. But the ones on the ground floor were boarded up, so he must get in up the balcony post and in at the best bedroom window. I guess his suit was not better off than it would have been out in the rain. But Karl was a sweet boy and wasn't going to have me in the pantry and himself on the wrong side of the door.

There was inside a musty fusty smell suggesting murder, suicide and avarice. We found some sacking, and it was damned cold in there, and we lay down there in each other's arms, and he told me about his horse Jupiter and made me laugh. This Jupiter was a fine-looking horse. He showed me his photograph. And Karl had him in the army. He was a German-Swiss and by the army I mean his military service, and Jupiter and Karl between them had cleared the board of prizes for style, performance, durability, reliability and an alert mind.

Karl also not only there in that Mrs. Humphry Wardish house, but, *passim,* told me about Luther. He was fond of Luther was Karl. And he told me how in bed one day Luther got thinking all sorts of thoughts about sex, and had visible temptations like St. Anthony. Do you know there is that picture of St. Anthony and his lovely girls? Now is it in the Kaiser Friedrich Museum, Berlin, or in London? I just forget. St. Anthony is looking rather pop-eyed and the temptations are mostly back-way on with fine posteriors that you could smack. That the Greeks made a temple to the backside of Venus, that anyone who knows what a fine thing sex is knows.

But this St. Anthony he is thinking that sex is simply *horrid,* simply horrid, and just a cause of stumbling and vexation. But instead of saying: You boys want to play cricket and keep on going long walks, and getting healthily tired, like the Walk-It-Off school of thought nowadays, he believed in prayer and starvation. He was a cenobite.

The early Christian catholic church was certainly puritan, like the catholics in Ireland. But the catholics in England nowadays trim their sails and walk oh so carefully-oh, and always set out to be so *simply healthy* and *patriotic*, according to the gospel of Fr. Martindale and Fr. Ronald Knox. You can follow up their line of approach. It is the forestalling principle active and rampant. Only sometimes, as forestallers are apt to, they trip up.

For instance, you are an average Englishman, a member of the established church, and you are having a talkie with a priest. You are interested. You are a prospect. Well then they think: You'll be feeling we catholics are Jesuitical, subtle, devious, and ultramontane—same as Elizabeth summed them up. Oh my dear chap—we aren't like that a *bit*. We're just simple *English* folk, like you and me, fond of home and not a bit *clever*. Oh not clever: 'I'm afraid I'm not very bright at putting things but we do feel that the dear Lord', etc. etc.

This is awfully funny, and sometimes I think if you want a quiet evening's healthy fun in front of the fire at home there's nothing on earth like those little twopennies of the C.T.S.

Take Bloody Mary for instance, and how everybody has always got Bloody Mary all wrong. It was that scheming sister of hers,

Elizabeth, in a way that was too-clever-by-half, and *no gentleman.* She was full of tricks, was Elizabeth, and *clever,* yes I'm afraid she was *clever.* But Bloody Mary was just a kind, sweet woman, like you or me, not clever a bit, just fond of a home life, and would have made a lovely mother if she'd ever had a kiddo.

Or take the inquisition. Oh *my dear*—that. And up go the eyes and hands and you feel it certainly isn't good form to mention the inquisition. Even if you do call it the *Spanish* Inquisition as if things were different in those parts. You know what Spaniards are. And this of course without prejudice to the fact that the church is one and the same, *semper eadem,* no matter where it crops up.

But it's hardly cricket you know, and, dash it all, not because there is anything in that old bogy, but because the-question-had-been-disposed-of-oh so many times. And what about Laud, and the Star Chamber? Yah. And what about all those brave priest-boys who came over here and got strung up and disembowelled under Elizabeth. And for why, please? Because she said they were traitors. Traitors, mark you. Oh she was the cunning one, was Elizabeth. And knew her public to a T. Just like Lord Beaverbrook. This flippant, frivolous, cold-hearted, and—yes *unnatural* woman. She knew the one thing the British public wouldn't stand for was a man, priest or no priest, that wouldn't doff his hat to

God Save the Queen. So she set about that they were traitors. But we catholics, in the simplicity of our child hearts, we know the truth about That Woman, and we know the truth about the inquisition. And weren't those times hard cruel times, and what about the civil code, wasn't that barbarous too? And anyway things are very different nowadays.

But alas! where the C. of E. is free to keep the good and discard the bad, the R.C.s have to swallow themselves whole, and the persecuting clauses are still on their books, although inoperative.

I admire the bishops of the Church of England and I often think about them and think they must get a laugh to see the way the R.C.s go round about trying like holy smoke to undermine them. First they'll try this and then they'll try that. But it's no good. You can't undermine the House of Lords and No. 10 Downing Street. And it's impossible to be a bishop of the Church of England and a fool. And most of them think more about the Church of England than they say. And what with this that and the other, and the State behind them, it would take more than Fr. Martindale to unseat them.

Well now, I was telling you about Karl, and the way he was telling me about Martin Luther that I never cared so-o-o much for.

Karl and I were having tea at Gunter's when this conversation came up and he said that when Luther got those visions like St. Anthony's he used to hop out of bed and stand there in the cold: 'You can imagine with what part of his anatomy exposed,' said Karl, beaming bright blue German eyes behinds spectacles. And Luther was this and that, and strong and single-minded, and not ashamed of his human frailties, which he tried to overcome these ways. And not afraid of his enthusiasms like you English. And your reformation.

There it was again. I was so vexed with his

allusion to Elizabeth and the bishops that I could not find a word to say. I felt I was going to choke. I was black in the face and the waitresses were walking up and down and everybody was drinking tea round about, quiet and contained like Christians. And suddenly I began to cry. I had to go out. It was worse than having hiccoughs in church. Karl put his arm round me and we walked up and down Bond Street and he said he didn't mind—didn't mind—and I wasn't so much not so much so English. Oh, were you ever so furious?

Karl and I met in many different places and many times, but best of all I like him and the others out in the counrty. Somehow I do not always find London sympathetic, the way I can be perfectly happy. Always there are some things that exasperate. I get much more furious in London than in the country. Oh beastly London—and yet at times so fine. Oh how I wish I had some money, then I could buy a haystack and go to sleep on it. No, Reader, this a symbol, and why should I not use a symbol if I like? This haystack is my ivory tower. Sometimes *plus que jamais je sens le besoin de vivre dans un monde à part, en haut d'une tour d'ivoire.*

Do you ever feel that way, you fool?

And specially at the moment my ivory tower takes not the form of a haystack but the form of a nice bed in a wide open lofty room.

There is. There are.

Oh but first of all why did I come out like that, I wonder, about the Church of England? It is always like this; really I find myself perhaps a little hypocritical the way I will not have anybody say a word against the institution. Now I think perhaps it is because it is such a very easy and already so very much knocked-about Aunt Sally, and it gets me so-o-o bored because really it is not that way. And I think soon we shall be saying: Really, some of the people who go to church are just as good as those who stay away. But actually I am not a Christian actively. I mean I am actively not a Christian. I have a lot against Christianity though I cannot at the moment remember what it is.

Oh I am so tired. There never was anyone so tired as poor Pompey at this moment at this page, at this very line, at this word. But wait, I will tell all before long.

But first, Reader, I will give you a word of warning. This is a foot-off-the-ground novel that came by the left hand. And the thoughts come and go and sometimes they do not quite come and I do not pursue them to embarrass them with formality to pursue them into a harsh captivity. And if you are a foot-off-the-ground person I make no bones to say that is how you will write and only how you will write. And if you are a foot-on-the-ground person, this book will be for you a desert of weariness and exasperation. So put it down. Leave it alone. It was a mistake you made to get this book. You should not know.

And it is not to be proud I say: I am a foot-off-the-ground person; or to be superior that I say: Foot-on-the-ground person—Keep out. It is to save you an exasperation and weariness that have now already hardly brought you to this early page.

But if you do not know whether you are a foot-off-the-ground person or a foot-on-the-ground person, then I say, Come on. Come on with me, and find out.

And for my part I will try to punctuate this book to make it easy for you to read, and to break it up, with spaces for a pause, as the publisher has asked me to do. But this I find very extremely difficult.

For this book is the talking voice that runs on, and the thoughts come, the way I said, and the people come too, and come and go, to illustrate the thoughts, to point the moral, to adorn the tale.

Oh talking voice that is so sweet, how hold you alive in captivity, how point you with commas, semi-colons, dashes, pauses and paragraphs?

Foot-on-the-ground person will have his grave grave doubts, and if he is also a smug-pug he will not keep his doubts to himself; he will say: It is not, and it cannot come to good. And I shall say, Yes it is and shall. And he will say: So you think you can do this, so you do, do you?

Yes I do, I do.

That is my final word to smug-pug. You all now have been warned.

So now I will go back again to play with the pet for a moment this delicious idea of mine, that is, about my haystack-under-the-eider-down tower of ivory.

First of all shall I have a haystack? Well idealized that might be quite good. First of all then we will consider the haystack. It stands up in a sunny field by the side of but out from a chestnut tree. So. The hay has been cut. Of course. It isn't imported hay in that stack. Well all the rest of the field, it is a very big field, it stretches away far and wide, and there on it are the swathes of white hay that have been left over. There it lies. So. There is a blue sky overhead and some white puff clouds bowling along in front of a summery wind. Not the sort you say as you crouch under the breakwater: 'I will say this about Shrimpton-on-Strand you can always get out of the wind one side of the breakwater or the other, or under the bathing machine.'

Well now into this picture empty of all human interest comes Pompey Casmilus. Here at last, she says, is the right haystack, the right moment, and the right solitariness. She climbs up the ladder, that was left did I say, on the top of the haystack. It is flat. And she pushes down the ladder because she doesn't care if she never wakes up again, but if she does wake up again she can jump. So I lie back on my ivory haystack and there is nobody else in the whole wide world and so I fall asleep. No dreams. No dreams.

Oh how fetid and debilitating London is to-day oh how I sigh for my ivory haystack.

Or let us now consider the wide open lofty room.

There is a very large house at the back of this very high wall I am walking along under. Hurrah, now it is off; this is the right beginning. I have heard of this very large house but I have never seen it or heard of anyone who has seen it themselves. Always it is: My aunt says that her stepdaughter's mother-in-law. You see—indirect and unsatisfying. Well, just now I was struggling along the Strand coming up from Fleet Street. At this moment Fleet Street just outside the *Daily Express* is up. Oh the brave music of a distant drill. Dear reader, the drill is not distant. Well, also there are all the usual smells, you know how smelly those parts are, so narrow, and that traffic, all those exhausts, and also the human beings, whose best friends still will not tell them, and to whom Personal Daintiness is not Rather Important, or not important at all.

What do you think of personal daintiness, Mr. Smelly?

'Do you offend?' cry the Americans. 'I'll damn well offend if I damn well feel like it,' say the English.

Harriet's favourite Johnsonianum:

LADY: Dr. Johnson you smell.

DR.: Madam, you smell, I stink.

FAVOURITE QUOTATIONS.

Favourite game for bedtime hour. Ian's (Margaret of Bedford's husband) He fell a victim to a horrible whore.

Hy. Adams: (Gibbon before the Gothic cathedrals) I darted a contemptuous look at the stately monuments of superstition. And Hy. Adams himself, of *horribile dictu:* Private Secretaries are servants of a rather low order.

I mean that vile torpedo Gaveston. That now I hope floats on the Irish Sea.

From the *East African Courier:* No more popular figure in Holy Orders ever motor-bicycled in Mombasa.

Venus . . . *quae quoniam rerum naturam sola gubernas.*

Pompey is an arrogant high hollow fateful

rider, In noisy triumph to the trumpet's mouth. (But this Pompey go bed on haystack.)

Oh and here is a nice one, oh, this is nice:

Around the tombs along,
The funeral paths among,
Deep shadowed elms
So lonely moans
The wind.

Les natures profondement bonnes sont toujours indécisées. (That's one in the eye for my sweet boy Freddy who says that is how I am, that is, *indécisée.)*

And here's another dirty one for the Church, from our own correspondence pages: Lonely One. Join a church or a hiking club or a debating society, refuse to spend your evenings along.

From the pages of the *Spectator*: Hogs' Puddings—Cornwall's exquisite reply to the continental liver sausage.

And from Highgate Police Court. Witness: I heard a faint puffing sound and three minutes later a policeman whisked round the corner.

Klassisch ist das Gesunde, romantisch das Kranke.

Darling Karl and his more-than-Luther-darling Goethe. 'Oh he is the man oh there is no man who has been so deeply and so *thoroughly* into everything.' Oh my sweet Karl, how I can see you now, though this is already a long time ago, with all of sleeping, dreaming, happily dreaming Germany in your blue eyes. Student of philosophy. At the University of Basle. At the University of Munich. At the University of London. At the University of Berlin.

Karl came to see us for Christmas. He brought his friend Pierre and for my aunt a flower in a pot, and for me? Now what do you think this sweet Karl brought his Pompey, on Christmas day, on Christmas day, on Christmas day in the morning? He brought

Pompey, chaps, a Translation of *Faust* in Two Volumes.

Oh but this is a dreadful translation of Faust, and I will tell you about it. Oh but it is dreadful and gives you the feeling that is making you strain away from Goethe and his great wide mind that had suffered so much, though I cannot help but think the body lived comfortably in that little *ville musée* of Weimar, where they still show you the *Todzimmer* where this Goethe laid his bones to die; and the *Todzimmer* of Schiller too, that is down the street and round the corner. Ah there is so much to be seen at Weimar, and the Germans are so extremely set on seeing things. It is wonderful the number of things they can see on a day's outing, when you and me would be sitting on the grass, in wicked English pride and arrogance, after living generations in the lap of security and got fat and sat back and wasted the inheritance of our forefathers; like Karl was saying later on.

But I see myself looking back since a long time, prancing round Weimar with darling Karl, that was so very darling when he had not got the ominous look on his face. And we see all the *Todzimmers*, and we see the pub and we trink-trink-trink, and then we get going round again, and it is a fine high sunny hot day in July, and by and by we have seen the statue the Germans put up to Shakespeare in Weimar. That certainly was kind of them, though Shakespeare looks funny-peculiar there in that *Unterdenlindengefühl* that is so much of Weimar. And Shakespeare is sitting there looking a little bit comic, and rather mocking and bewildered, with a nasty cynical wild look in his eye. That's why they've planted trees round him, that only the knowing Pompey might notice how Shakespeare was sitting there looking this way I have told you.

So presently Karl and I take a carriage. Where are we going-oh, sitting in this high sprung open equipage? We are now off to Schloss Tiefurt, bowling bouncingly along the white dusty road with the woods and fields on either side. And we are holding hands as we always used to on buses and on the underground and even going up Bond Street in England. And little Schloss Tiefurt stands back from the road. It is just a little Schlösschen, no larger than an English manor house, and there is a kind lady who receives. Will the kind lady receive? *Möchte die gnädige . . .* Oh she is kind and fat and comfortable with rather wicked eyes, not evil at all I do not mean, but: Oh you young people. There is that look in the eyes of the kind lady who receives. Oh you young people. And she brings us cups of coffee and cream, and cream cakes, and she is telling us the history of Schloss Tiefurt, and we are looking at the most beautiful statue of a gay raffish eighteenth-century laughing love child in stone, and Karl runs it over with his long sensitive fingers: *ja, ja. Das geht. Das geht.*

But in England we must quarrel, the quarrels must come. Always we were at quarrelling over this and over that. At the foot of the Duke of York's steps Karl said: I love you Pompey. It was December. There was snow on the ground. Outside the door of the *deutsche Botschaft* we kissed: I love you Pompey.

But later on the quarrels must come. Oh I love you so much Pompey, you are looking like a German girl with hair behind your ears. But oh the sad quarrels and the striving and fighting, it was our winter campaign of love and strife. And all up and down Hertfordshire from Hertford to Bayford through Monks Green woods over the estates of the Marquis of Salisbury, over Sir Lionel Faudel Phillips's fields, through the woods of Smith-Bosanquet, we fought and raged and also we laughed a lot and kissed and sang. But blacker and blacker grew the storms and the whole of our sky was overcast.

The English, the cruel cynical flippant frivolous pragmatical English of the upper governing classes, the enemies of philosophy and music and of every high abstract idea. With greed and pride and arrogance they possess the earth.

No no the English are not like this.

You scattered the bones of the Mahdi.

That must be done; it is something that has had to be done.

Cruel and ferocious and cunning opportunists that grind the stupid fat faces of your own common people that sacrifice everything of the spirit to the preservation of your famous *status quo. You scattered the bones of the Mahdi.*

But our poets. Never has England not given to the world poets of highest genius. But Karl, but Karl, these poets, from Chaucer onwards, the breed has never failed. How then can we be so base so materialistic so cynical savage and simian, so predatory so past praying for?

Well, chaps, there it is, what with Goethe and the Mahdi you see there was nothing for it but to part. And I remember at this time writing a poem about Karl and me that certainly had the truth in it—'and an icy crackling wrath, lies in rimy ridges on us both.'

And there is another poem I think of too that was when we met again by chance later in Berlin, as I shall tell you, and we could stand up free of each other's exasperation and irritation and aggravation and sickness and love, and we could look back at our other selves and think: *Where with venom all outpanted lies the slimed Curse shrivelling.*

And that is how I like to think of this and how I like to remember Schloss Tiefurt, and how I am always wishing to forget how the bones of the Mahdi were scattered, and I am even not at all anxious to read my Faust again because of the so-o-o bad translation and the false feeling of false classicismus about it. Oh that Helen that there is there. Oh the debased baroque, and the what-the-hell-was-the-man's-name—Winckelmannismus of his Klassizismus. And oh those 'bevies of beauteous dames' they are looking so small German court period 1760. Oh in this book that is such a bad translation there is that smell about it, that smell it might be a cheap excursion train-load of high browed kultur hounds. The train moves off from Leipzig. I think of it as Leipzig because I know that famous station, so we will say it is Leipzig. And the train moves off: *pünktlich Schokolade Zigaretten* southward bound for so many marks' worth of real Italian culture.

Oh it was those classical scenes in *Faust* and the bones of the Mahdi that finally drove the rift between me and that sweet boy Karl the way I have said.

While there is strife there is hope. That is a very profoundly Goethe idea, and I say this, this is my *amende honorable* for all that I said to Karl about he beloved Goethe in the heat of the wicked moment when he was saying: Myself I should have fought with the central powers for Germany, for Germany that cherishes everything in it of the truest civilization.

Ah that beloved Germany and my darling Karl. I too can see that idea of sleeping, dreaming, happily dreaming Germany, her music, her philosophy, her wide fields and broad rivers, her gentle women. But the dream changes, and how is it to-day, how is it to-day in this year of 1936, how is it to-day?

Now gentle reader you have been very patient very kind and forbearing indeed in this matter of Karl and myself, with hardly the look on your face at all that might be saying: No right-thinking girl would be so *crudèle* as to be so enervating for me, with all this stuff and nonsense, that no right-thinking girl would bring into the light of day to remember and tell at all.

So now you shall have some more nice little quotations for your scrap book. Or if you have no scrap book you can shoot them at your friends at your high-class parties and you may think you are lucky that you can just have them straight off like this and don't have to fit them into a speech the way I do for Sir Phoebus. If you don't guess the authors and care to write to me in confidence, enclosing stamped addressed envelope and a six-penny postal order for my ivory haystack fund, I will let you have the author's names. It will be a pleasure. Now, MORE QUOTATIONS

Let everything that creeps console itself, for everything that is elevated dies.

—— ——(guess the name) morte acerba fiore di giovinezza perduto gioie d'amore negate censo unica colpa rapito sepolcro disperso tanto non mi dolsero quanto la fama per lungo secolo contaminata ora che per vio si può sorelle romane rendete alle ossa il sepolcro alla memoria la fama ciò facendo gioverete alla giustizia eterna alla patria a me ed anco a voi.

The Dead Sea is very fortunately situated as compared with the German potash deposits inasmuch as its waters for practical purpose contain no sulphates. The sulphates though delightful from the theoretical point of view of the academic chemist have the habit of forming a large number of double salts, which would be the despair of many people.

Jessie: What is a love apple? A love apple is just another name for the tomato.

One of the greatest qualities which have made the English a great people is their eminently sane, reasonable, fairminded inability to conceive that any viewpoint save their own can possibly have the slightest merit.

Androcles—Roman slave who kindly removed a thorn from a lion's foot. On encountering the beast later in the Arena, it immediately fawned on him.

Take from the muscular stomach of a bird the number of people worth knowing in New York and I equal the remainder.

It is difficult to resist where nothing matters.

Thou water turnst to wine (fair friend of life); Thy foe to cross the sweet acts of Thy reign, distils from thence the tears of wrath and strife, and so turns wine to water back again.

If you have any old silk stockings you don't want will you let me have them? What for? To make clothes for the 'eathen.

Children are overbearing, supercilious, passionate, envious, inquisitive, idle, fickle, timid, intemperate, liars and dissemblers; they laugh and weep easily, are excessive in their joys and sorrows, and that about the most trifling objects, they bear no pain but like to inflict it on others; already they are men.

There was a young lady of Louth, who returned from a trip to the south, her mother said: Nellie, there's more . . .

And so we leave the cradle of Dordona amid the forest of huge-girthed oaks. Apollo speaks from the chasm of Delphi where Parnassus towers above; horned Hammon is sought among the sandy wastes of distant Libya; the phallic Baal upon the lonely heights of Peor in the Moabitish Land.

Trapped in the Hell of Modern Life they

fight . . . as you do . . . for the right to love. Enthralled—you'll watch this blazing spectacle of to-day torture the beautiful and the damned. Thrill as you See—Ten million sinners writhing in eternal torment—cringing under the Rain of Fire—consumed in the Lake of Flames—Struggling in the Sea of Boiling Pitch—toppling into the Crater of Doom—racked by agony in the Torture Chambers—Hardening into Lifelessness in the Forest of Horror! Plus the most spectacular climax ever conceived! Produced by Sol M. Wurzel. Directed by Harry Lachman.

Should I Marry a Foreigner? . . . You do not say, dear, if he is a man of colour. Even if it is only a faint tea rose—*don't*. I know what it will mean to you to GIVE HIM UP but funny things happen with colour, it often slips over, and sometimes darkens from year to year and it is so difficult to match up. *White* always looks well at weddings and will wash and wear and if you like to write to me again, enclosing stamped addressed envelope, I will give you the name of a special soap I always use it myself do not stretch or wring but hang to dry in a cool oven. My best wishes for your happiness, dear, I think it was very sweet of you to write.

My little Boy has Athlete's Foot. . . . This, little Mother, is dangerous. Do not play about with QUACK REMEDIES. Remove you darling's socks and shoes and immerse feet in hot water stir in three tablespoonfuls of white lead and the juice of a cucumber of the child is fractious apply a tourniquet. Be firm in treating childish ailments remember the psychological factor is incalculable. Pumice stone brought one Reader relief. Little children do not always have the right care and attention from both parents.

I cannot play this game of quotations one minute longer. I get bored. But I am far too quickly bored. Reader are you? Do you know how I think of you? I'll tell you. It goes like this and comes of having been asked to so many parties as I was saying about that insolvent Roman patrician because I am asked because I can be relied upon to talk to bores and keep it up and keep it up. Oh and so long as I get a free passage to the bar, and no questions asked, I'll do my best. I have my standards. I'll keep it up.

And sometimes it is as if you were at one of these parties that Larry gave. Well Larry was a ladylike boy with an elder brother called Henry that was a real solid man, that had a kind heart and was a big somebody in the musical world. Not the new brand-new-oh musical world that Harriet used to get so bored with, when she had that boy of hers used to trail her round the oh-so-new musicales, where the racket was so frightful with every man in the place telling you at the same time how he was done wrong by, and all his ideas cribbed, and himself not getting the rightaway like he ought, and all because the people who *Could* were lousy with commercial standards. Yes this was everybody's song at those musicales, and no wonder Harriet got thinking she'd have a change. Because Harriet is one of the Cans who Does, and pulls a fair income earned by hard and conscientious application, judgement, and tact too, because of the contributors she has to say No to, and yet not offend.

Well this Larry was full of clever ideas, and went across big, backed as he was by Henry's money to cover his risks. This Larry I'm telling you about—when I knew him and got asked up to his parties, there was good honest Henry by the bar *mum*, and there was the lion of the evening surrounded by Larry's old pals, and Larry himself running round and being oh so simple and full of fun, lots and lots of happy fun, and Larry just a brimful simple child of nature that never stooped to calculate. Oh no.

And I remember he was so funny, and when he used to sing as he used to sing, Reader, without provocation, just bursting from him, he used to sing chancy little folk songs—the chance being somehow or other he'd get some little twist or turn into it to make you know it was sex, sex, sex, made the world go round:

Bobby Shafto's gone to sea-ee, Silver buckles on his knee-ee, He'll come back and marry me-ee-ee—

With all that expression it would blow the

roof off, and in that song you'd know Bobby Shafto wasn't coming back to marry the girl, and the child would be just one more of those 3,432,521 illegitimate children they appeal for in the advertisements.

'Do You Know that there Are 3,432,521 illegitimate children in the U.K.? Please send a donation to the Secretary,' etc. That appeal came out in one of our papers, and when I showed it to Sir Phoebus he said: 'Hurrah! Who says England's going pansy?' Well, I thought that was funny coming pat back and not considered, so I laughed and told the assistant editor of that paper, and she said. 'Can you understand people like that?' Well yes, if you put it to me frankly like that I can understand people like that.

There was another song I used to love Larry to sing. 'Oh Larry Oh Larry do-o-o sing the Polish Mother Oh Larry do.' And Larry would turn to the lion and satellites and say: This tiresome child wants me to sing you The Polish Mother. And he would give a dirty look to Herman who accompanied him, and Herman, hastily putting his double Scotch out of reach behind the aquarium—pity the poor fish that never had a double Scotch—and remembering to smile the correct the obligatory Oh-isn't-Larry-Sweet smile would wipe his hands and place his fat little behind on the music stool and chase Larry through all the keys there are.

I am not musical, but Herman is, and Herman and his wife Rosa are friends of mine, and Herman with all his wonderful gifts, and the way he is always so busy he can't ever speak to one person at a time, but must always speak to twenty people at a time, each one getting one-fortieth of his attention, the other fortieth going on ahead to the next twenty people he'll be talking to, Herman says: of all the stimulating tasks he's ever had, that one of keeping up with Larry is the most stimulating, making the Mus. Bac. look as if he couldn't demean himself by trying.

Now Reader you shall have the Story of the Polish Mother, the Story of the song. First all the lights, except the one centring kind good Henry at the bar, were turned off, and the audience grouped itself around the lion, sighing and gulping. In pleasurable anticipation? Not a bit of it. Sighing and gulping because they'd been pushed into a huddle on the floor, where there wasn't really room anyway.

And: Oh David darling I do believe that's my drink you've got.

Well this Polish Mother, the song goes to say, it was I get the impression at the time of Kosciusko and the partitions, with the Russians all over the place, and forcing the peasants to have their babies baptized into the holy orthodox church, and all the ingenious cruelty that goes with it, and locking the cattle up without water, and beating the men to death with bludgeons that tried to water them, and spiking the babies and making the women look on. And over it all the Russian eagle, and the blaring trumpets and the dark night on-coming sky, lit up by burning ricks and cottages. Well all that isn't in the song, but that's the background. Freedom shrieked when Kosciusko died. But maybe the dates are wrong.

There was this woman sitting by the rick-burning firelight out on the open fields nursing her baby, and round about were the dead and dying. And the dead were the happy ones. And she is saying she can't nurse her baby, because she can't, because there isn't any milk to nurse him, and then she says to Christ to take the baby away.

Well that's all, but I needn't tell you how Larry made the hell of a lot of this song, and tore at his not so manly chest, and pulled the hair over his eyes, and the audience so damned uncomfortable on the floor, and just where you thought you could sit back and have a minute off, seeing it was dark and no one would notice, slap would come somebody's evening pump bang in the middle of your spine: Why sweetest was that you? Yes that was me. Oh look Jamie's kicked Nancy's bottom. Harold says Jamie's kicked Nancy's bottom, Rosa, Harold says Jamie's kicked.

Isn't Jamie a lovely boy. Oh Larry you are wonderful. Oh Larry you do the Polish Mother wonderfully. May I leave the room please Larry? Oh Larry, Jamie wants to leave the room. That certainly is a wonderful song. Mr. Merryweather, and I feel mighty privileged to get a new angle on Poland. I guess we in America don't know half what lies behind all these picturesque old countries. Oh isn't Mr. Higginbotham sweet.

Well, Reader, I sometimes get the feeling that you are one of those figures at Larry's party that Larry would take me up to after I'd had a word or two with kind brother Henry, and say: Oh here's Pompey, darling, you'll love each other. And Pompey would start right off the mark, Pompey No Weakness, was my motto that I lived by, like I was Danton.

But this was the old-fashioned London musical set I'm telling you about, with Germans and Austrians and Jews, and *lieder*, and Janet MacMurphy and miming and folk song, and now and then at Rosa's there would be a genuine ballerina.

There was one that always wore evening dress, very fat and tight, and a hat to go with it. And she had an American gynaecologist for a husband. He had a German name like they do, that I forget. He was naturalized U.S.A. and they had a flat in Curzon Street we used to go to, and Lottie (that's this ballerina) was certainly a good cookie was Lottie.

And we used to have little sandwiches with little hot sizzling sausages inside, and lots of strong black coffee to drink. And Lottie and her husband, I remember now his name was Horace Beit, had a little doggie they doted on.

Lottie couldn't do English very well, and Reader have you noticed how foreigners, when they always are wanting to be very English, have to use not just the right word but something even more so, like *doggie.* And when they got back to Berlin-Charlottenburg-Nussbaumallee *Nummer etwas* they say: Oh *no* Hansi, the real English say *doggie.*

Well this little doggie was a pomeranian that had broken front knees, or they were double jointed perhaps, and he was called Fifi, and they would say: Fifi, Fifi, Fifi. And Fifi would hurry up, and managing his front legs with real cunning Fifi would hurry up and shuffle across the room. And this was their child, their kiddo, and drank out of a real Jacobean cut glass goblet, and was real lucky to have found someone to be so fond of him and to cherish him, and take him car rides, though English people would say with those knees he would have been better dead.

Lottie was mean and thrifty and Horace was too, and fat, and underneath greedy and cruel; but to Fifi and Lottie he was their papa, their little big boy that was clever, and had a great big office where he made money, so that Fifi need never toil but could sit up like a lady on a fine cushion and drink out of a Jacobean goblet.

And one day I remember Lottie said: Pompey you should dress with more *chic.* So. And she put on me her hat and a coat with hanging sequin sleeves, and round my neck a piece of fur. And Rosa was there, and Rosa was looking at me with a look in her eyes that was a little bit begging me to remember that Lottie was important to Rosa, because of something between Horace and Herman. And I slanted my eyes at Rosa, and couldn't quite get the hang of that look, and I stood in front of a long glass and began to laugh silently.

Because it was funny. There in the mirror was Pompey, with the fur and the sequins and the hat, and behind on one side was Rosa bending forward anxiously, and behind on the other side was Lottie, with such a calculating one-and-three-and-six-one-and-nine-and-eight expression, and I thought in a minute she will say: Two and fivepence to you, modom. So I quickly went on laughing. And presently I said: Oh Lottie isn't it fun dressing up, you never know quite how funny you look until you put somebody else's clothes on, and people who are feeling full of wicked bounce should put somebody else's clothes on, and stand in front of a long thin mirror, with a Rosa and a Lottie beside, as if it was Christ crucified between thieves.

Like it was. Oh a green light shining through the dirty windows, on to a pink carpet, and the curtains were pink damask stamped with a floral dance of peonies, and the fringes were pink, and there was the dark face of Pompey with a long narrow head, and on top a hat like a turban would round, and a fringe falling to the fur band round the neck, and one hand outstretched to hold the gloves of green velvet, and the other hand up to the shoulder to throw back the sapphire sequins. And there was something that I didn't like, that I couldn't think, and then I thought: It's the gloves are wrong. So I threw them down and took up the goblet, that was Fifi's drinking goblet, and there was a pot of stewed tea standing on the mantelpiece. So I poured some of that into the glass and I went back and stood up in front of the mirror again, and tipped up the glass away from me so that it slanted into the light, and the tea looked like wine, with the light slanting through it. And that was a fine picture again, and I laughed and laughed, and looked to see the teeth showing through, and never shall I forget the fine picture that was. And my face was dark and brilliant and laughing, and Lottie's face was calculating, and then the calculations died, and the eyes were dead. And Rosa was frightened, and then the fright died and the eyes were dead. And I tiptilted the glass still further over, and I let the tea fall on to careful Lottie's carpet. I let the tea fall drop by drop till there was not any left in the glass at all, and I said: Blessed are they that shall not be offended.

Oh how glad I am I am not Lottie Beit, and how glad I am I am not Rosa, though I am fond of Rosa too, in a certain way, but not the way I am fond of Harriet and Topaz and Freddy and my aunt, and my sister and William and Anna and Josephine. I often think of Alice, and how she was glad she was not Mabel, and how for one dreadful moment she thought she was going to be Mabel. But that is just one thing we don't have to worry about. In our calm and reasonable moments we don't have to worry about that. There are hazards enough in life and death, but Alice can never be Mabel.

Just now my Aunt and my sister are away, and my aunt I will tell you about her, she is a lion. She is looking like a lion.

This what dear Frau Kramber wrote to me from Dresden after I had been staying with her and Emita. She was writing about her dog that was a lovely dog it stood four feet from the floor and was covered with long silky white hair. It had fine eyes and a gentle and dignified and sad face rather like Rembrandt's Jewish Rabbi. It had the name Dingo and was gently sad, bearing the burden of aristocracy and inbreeding as if it were an ancient Spanish animal. But so kind and not cruel at all.

Frau Kramber wrote to me to say that Dingo

had fallen sick, the complaint could not be diagnosed, he was sick. And by and by his long silky white hair fell off, and only a little on the end of his tail was left. She said: He is looking like a lion. That is a foreignism that is very vivid; they are bothered so by their teachers to remember that the participle is much used in present-day English and so always they are having to use it like that.

And darling Gertrude who writes to me from Berlin uses it too. She says: Why are you not writing to me it is a long time since I am not hearing from you.

There are so many people. By and by I will tell you about them all so that you will not have to say: Gertrude? We did not hear of Gertrude before, or, Freddy, who is that one? But I think the people must come in as they come.

And just now I am telling you that my aunt and sister are away, my aunt who thinks I am ten years old, and still a tiresome difficult and delicate child, as I was then. Though she loves me very much she does not say it, but she does, and I love her and respect and admire her. But of course my life runs on secretly all the time, as it must, and she has no idea that it does, and the way it does, and that I have been grown up in some ways since I was fifteen, in some ways since I was twenty-five.

My aunt will not let me stay along, in the house where I live with her. And when my aunt says that sort of thing, that is where I give way. Because really I think I should be very uncomfortable staying alone in that house, with no one to cook for me, or take in the things that come from the tradespeople. Yes I should be very uncomfortable. And again if she is to feel happy she must have her way sometimes, and why not on this point that does not matter to me? And on another point that does matter to me, I will not give way. But even there perhaps I will not make a fuss up about it either, but I will not say anything to her about it at all. And that is how it is that we live together it is now since I was four years old.

Oh what a fool I think Prunella was when she said to me: You want to get right away form that old-fashioned aunt of yours, Pompey, or you will find her an awful handicap, and your friends will laugh at you. It is not at all *chic* to live in a suburb with an aunt. But my friends think she is looking like a lion and that is that.

So now as she is away I am staying with Harriet and every weekend I go down to my aunt and sister who are staying at Felixstowe. I am enjoying this very much indeed. But every night it is later and later by the time we go to bed. We sit up and smoke and drink and talk; partly we talk shop. That is magazine publishing and colour pages, and the craft, guile and moral turpitude and essential timidity of directors.

This occupies a great deal of the time, because it is quite incredible how timid directors are, and how they cannot forget for one moment that the public must have this, and won't have that. But alas, what this is and that is, they never can quite decide. So they imagine two imaginary points, at an imaginary distance apart, and they fetch up at a spot half-way between these two imaginary points. And that's where they stay, and nothing will move them. And that's Policy that is.

So we discuss what we would give the public if there were no directors and no Mr. Copperbright to say to Harriet: It may be very artistic, but. And no Lord Victor Mohn to say: It's getting highbrow. Huff-huff. You must mingle with your public. Why not go up to the north of England and mingle with your public?

But of course all this keeps us up late.

Harriet has a flat in Clarence Mansions on the second floor. The furniture is silvered oak and the colour scheme—this reminds me of readers' letters. They write in 'from the north of England': I have taken a house, it is called 'Fairlight', it is semi-detached, can you give me a colour scheme for sitting room, kitchen, best bedroom and drawing room. But yesterday she had a reader's letter just this: Where can I get the china in your book?

Where a magazine is a book, you can reckon that's the public Lord Victor has in mind.

And that's the public which won't stand for highbrow nonsense.

Harriet's colour scheme is light beige walls paint and ceiling, horizontally striped brown and beige canvas curtains, canvas covered settee, perhaps it isn't canvas but it looks like that, and I am not an editor, or an interior decorator. And cushions made by her clever little boy cousin Kostin, some in very dark African nigger brown, and one in quilted glazed white chintz. And the silvered oak refectory table has a glass vase that looks like an ice block, with sometimes white lilies in it, and now I come to think of it the flowers are nearly always white. The bathroom has some green in it.

But now I am getting bored because I am not an interior decorator, and this has been a great effort for me because I have for so long not looked at the furniture at home that I find it difficult to look at furniture and remember to tell other people.

Harriet drinks a lot of China tea but she doesn't eat very much. She must be very strong because she does everything that would make me die. After I have been with Harriet for a day or so I get quite delirious with not eating very much and drinking China tea. It is then I get these so wonderful ideas about what we would do with the public if it wasn't for the directors, and Lord Victor Mohn and the press barons.

Charlotte came to dinner last night, she is Harriet's sister and has just got back from Greece where they were all brought up. Charlotte has a beautiful speaking voice and made me laugh about the difficulties she has had selling some of their property in Greece and how more than Levantine are the devious ways of Greek business men. It is very fascinating when she speaks Greek to Harriet suddenly forgeting me; I wonder what would have happened to me if I had pronounced my Greek like that at school; Posei*dōn*—that shows you. Harriet said how Venizelos was the only Just Man according to the ancient Greek standards that modern Greece had produced; but alas alas it's the Just Man gets the hemlock.

This is a world of ignoble animals, and the noble animals are hated by the ignoble, and are killed by them, or suffer afflictions, like that noble animal Dingo that lost his hair but nevertheless is noble and looking like a lion. And of course of course it is better to be noble and afflicted, in fact one can't help feeling sorry for the ignoble ones. It must be horrid to be Mabel.

There is one little thing that Harriet said that makes a picture I shall never forget. When Venizelos was in power he said he would not allow the dead to be carried in show-boxes through the streets. There was a great outcry about this because the people loved to dress up their dead people in wedding garments, and carry them in open coffins through the streets. It was a party. Tricked out in wedding finery you can imagine a dead old woman, withered and shrivelled, with white dress and veil and orange blossom. And the withered old man in respectable black clothes and a top hat. But perhaps they did not have a top hat. You see I have not seen it myself, I am only imagining it from Harriet's description, but she says they have a wreath placed on their heads, these dead old men, and the bearers tilt up the coffins.

And when Harriet and Charlotte were children, their Greek nurses used to lift them up so that they could get a good view. Well, think of it, the poor children, they would never see anything like that in England, where they actually sometimes bundle the dead into an oven and burn them up. So up went Harriet in her nurse's arms, and I can just see Harriet, aged four, with a stiff turned-up sailor's hat on the back of her head, and a sailor suit with a stiff pleated skirt, and legs, sturdy English baby legs, seeming to be stuck on to the skirt edge, it was all so stiff, and black-booted feet kicking in the air while nursie said: Look at the lovely dead people.

I am glad that nursie had a conscience and thought to do the right thing by her charges, or never would this story have come my way.

You can easily see how it is I am getting later and later getting to bed every night. Harriet can not sleep me at her flat, it is only a flat for one. So at last the last minute has come and we can neither of us bear another minute not to be in bed. But I think now that Harriet could always bear it but I no I cannot bear it because I cannot bear it.

Have you ever had a shock? said the funny doctor. I had at Hythe the time I was having flu. Now I was getting better from this dreadful flu, and one day, it was a bank holiday late in the evening, I went for a walk. I was very feeble but I could walk a little, very proud, and very weak indeed.

So round about Hythe and all through the streets of this little town, and up on the hills by the canal, there were pieces of paper, and there were cartons that had held ice cream and there were those little cardboard spoons that go with it. And there were newspapers and wrapping papers.

There was every sort of paper there, only the devil was there too, and he was not wrapped up in paper. And I had this vision of the fiend, and he was looking like—well he was certainly not looking like that great angel Lucifer that was so fallen, so changed, but was still that great angel that raised impious war in heaven and battle proud.

Oh no this was a very hateful sort of devil that had not in him anything at all of the dark mind of Milton soaring up over the dark abyss, very damned and noble. No this was the fiend that is neither like Goethe's Mephistopheles, that almost too impudent spirit of negation. No this was the fiend that is so, That is so, That is.

Oh I went too far for my walk that evening and I was wishing my dear Freddy, my sweet boy Freddy, was there to bring me home, and hold my arm, and be so loving and giving, as he is so sweet. But no, there was only the fiend, with his cartons of ice cream, and his little cardboard spoons and his oh. It was a dreadful vision that I had there of the heart of this fiend. And very stormisch and sad I was too, and full of the black night of foreboding, and when I came back to the hotel I was very profoundly disturbed. Very horrified and bristling with the breath of the frightful fiend was Pompey.

So I had my bath very hot and sat in it. I was so sad I could not even think to lie down. It was a very large bath, I sat there. My fringe was all cock-awry and the tears came running down my cheeks and fell into the hot water. And by and by I got out and got dressed for dinner, so sad so full of *désespoir* so much of nothing with a pain in my heart that was *sehr sehr aktuell*.

So I had my dinner, and next to me sat deaf Miss Musk that was often so funny. She was deaf, but perhaps now and then she could hear a little, so all the time she was making very particularly interested faces. Very enthusiastic indeed were the faces Miss Musk made, and you might be just speaking of the weather, but she would be looking so very much enthusiastically entranced, so quite enchanted, so eager and so intelligent, it was a pity you were not saying that the King was *affiancé*. But it was a pity.

But all through this dinner Miss Musk made up no face to meet imagined delights of calamity or joy. She was sitting looking at her plate, very preoccupied indeed, and Major Sykes, that sat over by the window with his papa and his mama, and his nanny was sitting at another table. This nanny had come to help his mama pack up to move away: Major Sykes had his dinner very early, and got up and bowed to us and went away. And my dear sister Mary was sitting opposite to me, but I could not speak, I could not eat the food, I was so choking all the time. I had to get up and go up to the lounge where there was nobody at all. And I think it is a good thing these was nobody there at all. So I sat in the chair by the window and I could no longer. There was nothing. I could no longer.

So presently my sister came in and brought with her the kind lady that was running the hotel, and she took me on to her knee. And presently they got this funny doctor that came in that said: Have you ever had a shock?

So I laughed and laughed and I said: I was born with a broken arm, and at three I had a way of getting suddenly very cold and quite, quite stiff, and having to be brought home in a milk cart. If there happened to be a milk cart, it was very fortunate indeed, for there certainly never was a cab rank when I was getting like this. So at five I had tubercular peritonitis and nothing but a trouble and an exasperation was I to my poor mama that was not so-o-o strong herself but indeed not at all strong. But I was an exasperating child and would not eat. My mama would feed me with a spoon: Now darling, this lovely lovely pudding. Now mama have some lovely pudding and now darling Patty . . . Patty bite, bite for mama, bite for daddy, bite for Mary, bite for Auntie. Oh naughty Patty, not bite for anybody. Not bite not bite.

Oh my poor mama how very *souffrante* you must have been with the Patty that would not bite.

So all these shocks were running through my head and I was laughing and laughing and thinking how I had told Freddy that in my pram they turned me round to face the way I was going because they could not bear to have me sitting up looking at them with that old-fashioned look of cynical hauteur, the way they were bumping me up the kerbs, that would have said if I could speak: Go, sweep a crossing.

Now I will tell you some more about my Aunt that is like a lion. I think of her as the lion of Hull. She was born in Newcastle. When my mama was a girl she was being rather romantic, and so she made an unsuitable marriage. My aunt used to say: If your grandmother had lived your mother would never even have met your father. And then I think where would Pompey have been, where would that Pompey have been that has her hat on the back of her head, and her fringe awry that is looking always like Eddie Cantor and feeling like a Roman scandal?

And at this time I had a nanny that was William's sister, that had run away from home and so she had to be a nanny, but very vigorous and affectionate was this nanny, that was called Elizabeth, and very strongly indeed she took to my mama, and very strongly indeed she raged against my papa that was to her villain of the villa. She would not have one good word said for my papa but was always shaking her head and saying: If the truth were known, and: It can come to no good. And: There will be trouble. So very soon I began too to rage very furiously against my papa. I sat upright in my baby-carriage and wished mama hadn't made such a foolish marriage.

But now I think that for the husband as well as for the wife, an unsuitable marriage must be a very dreadful thing indeed and so I have a feeling for my papa that was not at this time at all.

But my papa could not stand it, he just could not stand it. Perhaps he was a weak man, but always he was being frustrated. First when he was a little boy he wanted to be in the navy. But no that dragon that was my paternal grandmother, she would not hear of it, because an elder brother was drowned. Setting out to sea from Hull, and making for Riga, he was drowned before he had got beyond sight of land. So this little boy Charles, he must not go into the navy. So presently he must go into the shipping business that my grandfather had. But oh it was all dust and ashes and long long hours of boredom for that Charles. So then the war broke out that was the Boer War, so my papa that was then in the Yeomanry he must, he would, he must go to the wars. He must go in khaki with the Duke's son and the Cook's son off to Table Bay-o. But then no he *must not* go.

There was, chaps, a combination against him. That female dragon my grandmother was very much against it, she was very much against it indeed, and she prevailed upon my mama to prevail upon my papa. So sure enough he did not go, and sure enough there was, certainly yes certainly, there was trouble. Because suddenly my papa could not bear it one moment longer. So off to sea he went. Yes my papa he ran away to sea after the war was over and he left his wife, who was already so tired and ill, and left his Pompey who was such a baby for having such a funny look in her eye that made you feel you weren't quite sure after all if it was.

'Off to Valparaiso love Daddy'. For many years now that is all we were hearing about it and about, and so as we never knew when he was leaving, we never knew where he was. It was very very disturbing and unusual these post cards that we were getting 'Off to Valparaiso love Daddy'. And a very profound impression of transiency they left upon me.

So then it was, and how it was, that my Aunt the Lion of Hull came to live with us. She must look after mama, and she must look after Mary, that is my elder sister and she must look after this Pompey that is such a desperate character.

This lion has a very managing disposition, is strong, passionate, affectionate, has enormous moral strength, is a fine old Fielding creation, Her hair is now iron grey. It stands up on end. It stands up straight. It is hair that has suffered forty years' crimping with red-hot irons but still it is standing up on end.

As a child I used to lie in bed and watch my Aunt, a thing she could not bear. She would glare into the looking glass, her eyes would flash, she would seize the tongs and screw them down red hot into the heart of the hair. She would fall upon the hair, pounce upon it with red hot irons.

I think I can still smell the hair burning upright like a holy Christian martyr. 'Tarnation take it.'

I think that is exactly the way the Roman

executioners were speaking, professional pride outraged, when Blandina would not sacrifice to the idols. 'Tarnation take it,' the echoes come back to me now and I am still living in the same house. There are only two of us here now. My sister Mary teaches school and comes home for holidays. When there are no holidays there is only this darling Lion of Hull and myself.

Now Reader you see how dangerous it is for a novelist to get in the family way. There's no end to it, and before you know where you are you're heading straight for those cradle-to-the-grave novels that never let you out under three volumes.

But I can pull up when I want to. I am the cleverest living Pompey. I can pull up as I pulled up when I got talking about Kismet, and the way he went round eating off the walls and houses of Cornwall, and the crops too and every living vegetable.

I have told you all this to show why it comes about I have a feeble constitution and the onus of keeping early hours and eating good plain English food and lapping milk at regular intervals. And these things I never do. I should be bored.

But sometimes when you have been done out of your sleep-o you get morbid, gentle Reader, you get morbid and cross.

When I was coming back from Germany once, we had crossed night time from the Hook, and somehow or other something broke down, we got turned out early at Harwich, and there was this trainload of British that had been done out of their sleep-o, and turned out early into a cold cold train, with never any breakfast and not even an early morning cup of tea. And there was this trainload of British. And there was never anything on earth so cross ever.

That is what happens when you are done out of your sleep-o and the simple pleasures of a well ordered life.

And when I went into that railway carriage there was that atmosphere of frosty fury that only the British can throw off, and only when they have been deprived of their sleep-o and their early morning cup of tea. And there they were, men and women, sitting up stiff, with black wicked temper, and that don't-touch-me look, though they were all touching each other, and lapping over, being more to the carriage than was right, owing to the something that broke down.

And no matter for the crowd, there was still one seat in the corner that was empty.

And for why? It had above it the writing 'Reserved'.

So the train was just starting, so in that seat I sat down, and the icy rimy wrath of the British atmosphere in that carriage curled round my head. And did I care when the train went out of the way they hadn't thought it would, so that the icy furies opposite went up to Liverpool Street Station backing the engine, that had so-o-o carefully chosen the seats facing the engine? And I thought: I admire this icy British temper that can be so cross, and yet remember to leave the reserved seat for the latecomer, who would be still more cross, having got hung up in the customs. But actually of course he never turned up at all. And I hope he caught the relief train, and I hope he had a corner seat facing the engine, like I did.

It is when I get morbid and cross from lack of sleep-o that I play this game I was telling you about, this game that is a twin game to the haystack's ivory tower of bliss.

You are suddenly not in London or any town any longer, but you are walking along a long straight road, it might be in France, it might be by Utrillo, and there are trees, and there is this long straight white road, and you wonder how many more miles, and you think: Boots boots boots boots moving up and down again there's no discharge in the war, but there is nobody else in the whole long length of that road, and perhaps there has never been anybody else there at all, it is quite deserted, and the countryside either side is a flat plain, like it might be stretching out to the sea over saltings and a samphire, and the road is dyked up, and there is a white stone wall banking it back and running alongside.

And so you go on and on.

And presently the trees give way and there is nothing but the road, and presently the road gives way and there is nothing but a track, and presently the track gives way and there is nothing but this marsh and samphire beds, and underfoot it is looking caked and hard, there has been no tide seeping up a long while.

And presently you know to turn to the right across the saltings, and there sure enough is the house. It is a high square white house and has outbuildings and barns lying low, and a stone wall going round it to keep the wind away, and now it is getting dark and there is an enormous strong wind suddenly blowing very proud and revengeful. And you will only get there just in time. And you go in through the gate of the wall, and you shut it behind you, and you go up the pathway that is bordered by trees all blown one way in spite of the wall, and so you come to the heavy door that has a stone porch, that has stone steps leading up to it, and you unlock the door and you go in and shut the door behind you, and bolt it, an inside there is a wide stone hall and lights hanging down perfectly steady. Though the wind is now roaring round the house it cannot get under the door.

And you go up the stone staircase that has shallow steps, and up and round, and there is a long oblong dining room with food set out on the dining table. And the food is, first there is grouse *en casserole* and potatoes baked in their jackets, very hot and fresh. And then there is a beer to drink, and then there is mushrooms on toast, and then there is figs fresh picked, and then there is this cool beer to drink. And there is a little fire burning in a basket in a large stone fireplace, and you sit there beside it for a while and watch the sky getting darker in the great sash windows, and the sea is out there, and the wind is roaring, it is roaring for its own pleasure.

And so by and by you go to the bathroom, that is a large square bathroom flagged with stones, and the bath is a large stone bath, and the water comes crashing into the stone bath hot and foaming, because of the salt in it, it is brackish water, and you get in. It is so deep, and the bath is so big, you can float. And the light is hanging down perfectly still and burning steadily, and you have a loofah and a bath tablet of *fougère* soap-oh, and you scrub and wash carefully all over, and you dry yourself with hot towels standing on a loofah bathmat that is prickly to the feet and not slimy the way rubber bathmats are. And you rub, and when you are dry you put on a dressing-gown that is made of thick dry very thick towelling, it is heavier and drier than a bath sheet, and you put on slippers that have linings of this same heavy towelling.

And now the moment has come for you to have your lovely sleep-o. And you go quickly along the passage, and there are doors to the right and left, but the door is at the end of the passage, and there is the lovely bedroom where you are going to have this lovely sleep-o.

And it is dark in here now, but not quite dark, there is still some little grey light coming in at the wide open sash windows, and there is no rattle or movement at the panes, though the wind is roaring for its own pleasure outside, and the sky is streaked with this little grey light, and there is the sound of the air rushing and roaring for its own pleasure.

And the bed is a high bed, it has no foot board and no head board, it is high and flat, there is only one pillow and the sheets are turned back, and the bed is standing in the middle of the room. It is a large square flat high straight hard bed, the sheets are white and dry and fine as dust. And so you kick off the slippers, you throw off the dressing gown, you climb up into the bed and lie down flat. Ah this is the lovely dark room, and the air is in and about and in through the great open windows, and the grey light is in the dark sky far away.

Ah night space and horror, keep my dream from me.

Now, Reader, I am going on my holiday to Germany. This is already several years ago. I will say the boat train to Harwich, and this is not getting back at the London and North Eastern Railway Company but I will say their boat train *is quick.* The Lion my Aunt of Hull, like I said, saw me off. First we had dinner at the Great Eastern Hotel. They have slap up joints of meat there. Already Food Matters. Already there are Germans seriously eating.

About the boat train to Harwich I shall have something to say later, Miss Casmilus. But about that branch line to Felixstowe, that is not quick, I shall have something to say now. Oh no, it is not so quick at all.

First there is Ipswich, then a long time later there is something that sounds like you'd left Ipswich. Left *Ipswich,* my dear fellow? Wait. Then there is *Something Roads,* that's just plain Ipswich back again, to take the wicked pride out of you. Then there is Orwell.

That name comes back to me. Orwell. And very pretty Orwell is, but don't go rushing the beauty of Orwell, take it in tree by tree, and count the daisies on the flower beds. There they move the train up and down, so that every bit of the platform gets its whack and everything is fair and no back answers. Take a look at Orwell and remember, you'll see it again on the back journey. Orwell's all right there's nothing wrong with Orwell.

And then later there is Trimley, poor after Orwell—but scheduled for ten minutes' observation to help you get hold of the idea that Felixstowe, like I said *Felixstowe,* comes next.

That is Felixstowe Town. To the Ultima Thule of Felixstowe Beach, Reader, I have not penetrated, preferring to run along the esplanade and back in time for a good English dinner, that has got none of the Continental nonsense about it, like I said the Great Eastern Hotel has been debauched, stampeded and contaminated by trans-German-Ocean food fancies.

At Felixstowe dinner is on a higher plane. Very spiritual. With pink Shape to follow, very Platonic. Like it was a This World carbon copy of A Great Idea.

But now this boat train that is running me into Harwich very swift and serious, this boat train that is full of German nationals this boat train is a fizzer, and already I am thinking that my aunt and Baldur Löwen, that came full of *Heimweh* to see me off, are already a long time since and away.

Ich fand etwas zu Berlin was mich anheimelte. Well that's pretty punk I guess, but when I learnt German we were put to study German plays, and our German lady made us get the bits by heart, very free and easy they were, and o.k. so long as you stuck to the text, but limiting the conversation when you got mixing with natives. For when life has to copy art to that extent, it certainly cramps the daily necessities of travel, with its recurrent problems of food, housing, trains, trams, *Untergrundbahnhof* and bye-bye.

That play was *Der lebende Leichnam* I shall tell you about later. Very fine and high-class; it was by Tolstoi, done into *deutsch* out of *russ.* And that's what I mean when the hero says *er fand etwas bei den Zigeunern das ihn anheimelte.* Well you have to think: Now *Zigeunern, das geht nicht,* and you have to think and change it round to suit. And that's where this method trips you up. For sometimes, like we all suffer from brain fag times and again, you might let it run on, and it might give a wrong impression, because, when the accent's o.k. and the words are o.k., and fine current German, you get held responsible for the meaning. It's not like showing off to your English friends, that don't know German anyway, and get thinking you do, the way you run on so fluent *das heisst fliessend.*

Well listen to Harry. Who'd have thought poor old Harry was good at languages. It must have been that he was being good at them all the time we never knew, and not just a plum halfwit like we thought, but just being good at languages. Like we never knew. Well, come on Harry, say us some more. See?

So here was I set down in this boat train going to Harwich. And by and by we got to

Harwich and on board. It was a nice comfortable cabin I had, and my lady cabin mate never gave me a moment's trouble, going straight off to sleep-o like a baby. I am never sick crossing the North Sea, but I always take a flask in case I am, and to give me confidence, and if you don't drink it then it comes in handy later for coffee and ginger beer.

I often wonder what would happen if you mixed stout and brandy, like that drink they have, the men tell you it is a *man's drink* and not for women in any circumstances. It is called Black Velvet. Well this black velvet is mixed half and half of stout and champagne, and I dare say if you were given that cheap sweet champagne as happens at some twenty-firsts, I name no names, it might be a good thing to send the butler scratching round for a Guinness.

But if you did that, people might get set against you, and what's more you might not get asked to the wedding, that always, with cousins and other relations you have to give gifts to, comes so close along on top of the twenty-first. Well if you weren't asked to the wedding, you wouldn't have to give a present, so though you would not get the chance of another dollop of black velvet on the hostess, you'd be no worse off.

And in a thoughtful doze I passed quickly through the customs at the Hook. And still dazily dreaming of black velvet, I got on to the train.

The Hook at 5 a.m.—or was it 7?—very early, very fresh, is a long deserted platform. Whenever I travel that way I always seem to be the only person: Well fancy, you going to Berlin? Well I never. No, we haven't had anyone for Berlin not since—Hi George, when was it we had that last passenger for Berlin, the old gentleman that wore a dundreary whisker, and was so generous with his money?

Curiously deserted and grass-grown the platforms of the Hook, but very spacious and comfortable the train. Five or seven o'clock in the morning, whichever it is, is very curious, very early, for one whose rising is habitually later than usual. How later than usual one is apt to become, only the Lion of Hull knows.

That lion, my aunt, has very sad late habits. At night time she has habits that are a genuine bit of Old Fielding. No light late night-cap of Horlicks Is Helping Her Now, but the cold game pie she found in the larder. That larder, stocked by my aunt, is also a perpetual surprise and treasure trove to my aunt, though surely *she*, and certainly neither myself nor Mrs. Green the car, put that game pie there yet: Why Pompey, here is a bit of old game pie in the larder. Will you have some for supper? This is now already perhaps twelve o'clock at night. Why no, Aunt. I can't say that I just fancy old cold game pie. Not to say just fancy. You go ahead, Aunt, I said you go ahead Aunt, you'll enjoy that old cold game pie. But I'll just have a mug of hot milk and a shake of Ovaltine. So much feebler are we nowadays, the younger generation.

With admiration and ever fresh wonder I watch my Aunt. She puts the game pie on the table, and finds some other remoter treasure trove a bottle of beer. Then there are those crisp new crusts of bread. Already my aunt has the feeling: Oh lovely meal-o. Oh blessed food.

She sits down and takes a little sauce with the game pie. She props up the newspaper and reads from the legal columns. There is great joy there for my aunt, for there on the legal page Somerset House in all its black delinquency has been caught napping, has been found against by some despairing claimant.

Ha ha, that is a moment of great joy for my aunt, for she has often told me: Were any private business concern run on such lines they would all have been bankrupt long ago, as I told the Inspector. Yes, she told the Inspector. And she has told me now already many times. So now she is crunching her old cold game pie and reading the paper, and seeing Somerset House cast down in all its piracy and black predatory heart of pride.

Sometimes my aunt reads out every bit of her income tax form aloud. With snuffling and sobbing in the throat, for the wickedness that is set down there, and fury in her old lion heart, and biting of nails, and thrashing of tail, up and down the house she goes, and scratching and scuffling round she goes to the cupboard low down where the receipt skewer lodges. Every receipt we have is impaled on this mighty skewer, and there is more rustling and scratching, and finally the receipt conclusive is produced, and now bursting with righteous triumph she sits down to write to James. This James is a cousin of hers who has a high-up post in the wicked heart of Somerset House. This James he is very clever and very conscientious, and very hard working. Never mind, if he is sometimes seeming a little severe, for life must be all work, and he is also a socialist of the old good Huxley-antimacassar period, when it was the acme of man's rights to work twelve hours a day, and go to a night school free for the remaining six, with six hours' bye-bye on as hard a bed as could be found. And this is the life he has led himself. He is very severe, but also very kind, and he advises Somerset House if a Case Lies. He is on the legal side is James, and he is always good to my aunt, and takes up the cudgels on her behalf, so that I believe the local income tax officials are frightened when they see my aunt approaching, because they know she's got a brainy irascible Old James up her sleeve.

But my Aunt has difficulty in putting herself on paper. First she has to make a rough draft, which she reads over to me. It is very funny, and very indignant, and very indistinct, like someone is choking they are so cross. And always the word position comes in, because my aunt never knows how that there is only one 's' in this exasperating word. But somehow all the same the letter gets written, with all its i's dotted and its t's crossed. And then there is some more fuss up, and another roaring and lashing because the stamp she put under the bronze statuette of Van Dyck is no longer there. But finally and at last the letter is posted, and then there is a moment when you are almost deafened it is suddenly so quiet.

I was thinking about this, and especially about my ant and the old cold game pie, and the pickles and a bottle of beer, as the train left the Hook. And oh how curious and disembodied one feels at that time in the morning, and already the dew has not yet gone from the fields, and Holland is looking all dewy-wet, and the fields have mists curling over them, and the cattle stand muffled up to the you-know-whatever-it-is, like Peter Graham's Head of Cattle. And I often wonder if for him the hoofs of cattle were especially sacred, so that there was always a nimbus of mist around them, or if perhaps they were for him impossible to draw, so there was always this nimbus of mist, or a concealing blanket of heather.

My aunt and mother had a painting master when they were children at school at Malvern. That is a very long time ago. I think of them at school at Malvern when the Franco-

Prussian war was crashing over Europe, and *Boule de Suif,* that is how I think of that period. But this painting master he used to have his pupils copy pictures, then he would come round and put in the difficult bits. He was very kind. His name was Ernest Cooper, but never did the canvas have *Ernest Cooper* in the corner, but only the name of the pupil. So when my mother copied *King Charles's Spaniels,* and Ernest did the dog's faces, he got only the pure satisfaction that he had helped those dogs round a tight corner. On the canvas was just my mother's name which was Rachel Silver.

And my aunt was set to copy Landseer. Oh it was Landseer this and Landseer that, and Lanseer up the stairs and in the front hall, and in the dining room it was *The Monarch of the Glen,* as tasty a bit of venison as ever got hung. But finally my aunt was set to copy some sheep. There was a fold and lots of sheep inside, just an impression of a mass of sheep. And then there was one sheep that got looking out of the fold, as if it had heard something calling it a long way off. And it had on its face in my aunt's canvas, that must have been the day Ernest Cooper got sick, it had on its face that expression of low cunning like you get on a company promoter's face. And a little to the off-side was coming on an expression of shifty fear, as if what it had heard a long way off was the hue and cry of the shareholders that weren't going to stand for any more of it. No Sir.

It was clever the way my aunt had got all this on to one sheep's face, but it was there so plain that my grandfather put his foot down.

And that was the end. And I think too now that it was a good thing about that sheep, and my grandfather putting his foot down, because already every single canvas had been framed in heavy gilt and hung up round and about the house, and not one of them had ever been allowed to go astray, they were all there to muster, including *Faith in the Arena* by my mother, with a lion in the background that unlike Dingo was certainly not looking like a lion at all, and *For the Queen and Old Ireland* that was a young soldier with a bandage on his head, and a look in the eye that was coming out of the bandage that boded no good to the family that harboured him. And *The Blacksmith's Forge.* And this large canvas: there were a lot of horses and a man lying on the belly of his horse, that was all shot away, and the man you could tell was dead. And on the man's belly was his dog, his doggie, that was putting his paw on his face, and lifting up his head. It would make you cry. And there were two officers. Yes I remember now, that was Napoleon, and that was the retreat from Moscow and that one was called, let's all have a good cry, *Man's Best Friend*. But what was man's best friend?

Was it the dog, or the horse, or Death that cut him off from all the cruel hungry frost and snow, and iron rations gone seven days since? That is where you can take your choice, you can do what you like about it. Work it out for yourself.

These are the things I was thinking of, and by now we have got to Hanover, and very lucky I was to have all these things to think about, seeing that the North German plain isn't much to look at, and the North German business-man faces you get in a second-class carriage going to Berlin are better not looked at. And here we are at Hanover and *Schokolade* and *Zigaretten und bitte wie lange ist hier Aufenthalt.*

I was thinking of Mr. Ernest Cooper, and how kind he was, and how clever, with one touch for elm trees and another for oak trees, and another for weeping willows, and something quite different for pollards, and all the time nothing to show for it all, just stifling anonymity, and no satisfaction, no revenge, when plop I got shot on to another line of thought: Why the hell does one come abroad for holidays after you don't get school holidays any longer? The awful cramping weariness of long journeys, and no sooner there than back you have to come again. What it is like is this. It is like you were an elastic band hooked on to *Bahnhof Zoo* at one end and stretched right over to Liverpool Street Station at the other end, and gradually, oh at first you feel so tensed you could die, but then bit by bit the nearer you get to *Bahnhof Zoo* the less tensed you get, till you're just about ready for tea when you get in to Berlin. Phew.

That way I have never approached before. Before I was coming from Dessau and in to the *Anhalter Bahnhof,* but this way coming straight from the North Sea, like a great rushing-up tidal wave, this is almost as if you were still in Holland.

Why I had come was. Why Harriet had got a new paper given to her and had shot up over it, and just couldn't couldn't anyway get herself off for a holiday. So Harriet is phony about holidays, and goes chasing off home to Greece via Brindisi and back again in the fortnight, having spent the intervening days, the ones in Petras, coping with uncles and aunts of pronounced irritability and incompetence, and coping with them and with very very difficult and obscure business transactions that only Greeks know about. Greeks, Jews and Levantines. Does that paint a vivid picture of nefarious complications? I bet it does. So Harriet would come back from her fortnight and have to go to bed, and even then it would be quite two or three months before she was quite better from it.

So this time I thought: I'll go off again to Berlin and stay with those people I stayed with before that have now moved to Berlin from Dessau. They were called Eckhardt.

Though by this time I wasn't so-o keen on seeing the Eckhardt *famille* again, but they were the only people I could think of to go to at a moment's notice, that was all I could give them. So Franz Eckhardt the husband met me at the station and they was living in Halensee now, so off we went, Pompey feeling very distrait and wrapped up in tearful thoughts of the hard lines it was for Ernest Cooper not getting his name on those canvases.

These Eckhardts, I remembered now too late, were of English extraction, back a long long time ago. So being of that dominant English strain, they had kept over all this time the idea fixed and British that one language was enough for any Christian, and being good at languages like poor Harry, was o.k. for commercial travellers and the funny boys in the Berlitz schools, and it could stop there.

So there you see how it was they didn't speak English, and how peculiar it was for a Herr Doktor living in Berlin, with a government educational job and the kadet school behind him, to have never got a grip on English. But that was the sort of thing I would do, go and stay with the Eckhardts that couldn't say a word of anything but *deutsch*.

I wanted the Eckhardt boy to stop and give me a drink. I felt real unearthly by now, that I might go up to heaven any minute, wafted straight up and no visible means of support.

There didn't feel to be any weight in me at all. I seemed just pure spirit held down to earth by a tweed travel coat. My God that boy never so much as batted an eyelid in my direction as we swung past the café bars. Oh did you ever want a drink so? Then suddenly providence whispered in my ear: You got a flask, so I kept smiling smiling all the way after that till we got there.

This Eckhardt I couldn't take to him at all, he was a little skimpy thing that rather put me off. But his wife Ludmilla was o.k. so far as I could made out, and so far as I could remember. And I suddenly guessed I'd taken an awful risk coming off along to Berlin to stay with these Eckhardts that I hadn't seen for some years, and then only for one of these fortnights they throw to us at the office. And I thought: What aeons of boredom you can get into a fortnight, and if there wasn't something offputting about Herr Snooks, I would have put my head on his shoulder and cried and cried. That's how I felt when we got to that high-class *Wohnung*.

Ludmilla met me at the door, and she'd got tears running down her face. What did I say It was All Up. They gave me cold sausage meat and coffee, and bits of things that looked like gherkins, and then I gathered that the kid was queer. So they took me in to see her. This kid was called Trudi. Well Trudi certainly looked the end was in sight. There she sat up aged four, and she had circles under her eyes you'd think she'd had nights of drinking behind her, and she was casting down her eyes and twisting one finger round another. Oh I hate to see a kid that way, so I said: Oh let the kid alone I guess she's frightened at me she don't rightly remember me at all. But they badgered her to say: How-do to Tante Pompey, and she wouldn't so I went out, and later when I got the poor kiddo alone, she was quite all right and said: Now Tante Pompey wash up. It was in German, mind you, Reader, but I got the hang of it enough to lay off and say: Tante Pompey velly solly no speakee Chinee. That child was neurotic all right.

So we were going on, they meant it to be the next day, to the seaside, to a country place on the Baltic called Neuesdorf, right up beyond Danzig, so of course as the kid was off her feed, we had to hang about in Berlin. This suited me fine. Ludmilla was all right once you got her along. Baldur Löwen, that German I knew in London, had seen her photo and said she looked *hysterisch* and was her husband a small-stature man of under five feet? Well that Baldur certainly had clever ideas. Well I said yes, he was a proper little rat. So he nodded like he knew it all and said that was the reason, and there was nothing to be done about it anyhow except, to throw the little ones back and stick out for a full size like it was the Göring boy.

I was too well bred to pursue the conversation further, with Baldur Löwen looking like he knew all the answers. But his remark came back to me sitting opposite Ludmilla in Kempinsky.

She certainly looked all on edge and was always coming out with bits about *unser liebes Vaterland*, and Our Happy Family at the *Wohnung*, and all cosy and warm-o, like it was protesting too much, like it was what all Germany was suffering from, the *männlicher Protest*, that they invented themselves. Very subtile this was and a great deal too warm and cosy-o for my taste.

So I rang up some Jew-friends of mine that lived out Charlottenburg way, and went to see them. This was before the Hitler campaign, or leastways it was just getting on the way, so that these Jew-friends had already had the black *Hakenkreuz* scrawled up on their gateposts. But at any rate they were sound enough, with a weather eye out for self-preservation and not a sign of neurosis there. Very sound and objective and sensible after the neurosis in the Halensee *Wohnung*.

Later on I took Ludmilla to the modern art gallery, and who should I see there but that sweet boy Karl. Now this was surprising, because Karl by rights should have been in Switzerland and nothing was further from my thoughts. When there, looking at *Der Turm der Blauen Pferde*, was Karl. Well that cheered things up for me, and I guessed the tide had turned in my favour. We were *ganz platonisch* by this time, understand me, but off we went dancing and swimming and going to Potsdam, where we sat in a café and talked for five hours, and that was after we had slipped round *Sans Souci* in felt slippers, and laughed till we cried, while the old guide boy was getting furious and saying his piece all the time.

The Eckhardts asked Karl up to dinner at the *Wohnung* and Herr Doktor talked the fuedal system at him. Certainly that Her Doktor took ten for boredom every time.

I soon got thinking how much nicer Karl was in Berlin than what he was in London. He was easy and laughing, and made me laugh, and there was none of that censorious grumbling about the British and how incorrigibly flippant and materialistic they were, and how deeply arrogant and predatory. No Karl certainly was a sweet boy that time in Berlin. So sweet was Karl that when I got to Neuesdorf I could not stand it for more than four days. That is the truth. But it wasn't all on account of Karl, oh no, that Eckhardt neurosis got more and more pronounced. Always Trudi was having her hands smacked at meals for putting them on the table, and then she had to be told a fairy story, and all the time it was just the one fairy story that I got nearly by heart. Reader, it was The Wolf and the Seven Little Kids, and when it ended up *Der Wolf ist tot Der Wolf ist Tot*. Hurra, hurra, hurra, the blood lust and ferocity on the infant face of the infant neurotic was something more than I could stand.

And there was another one she would allow sometimes to be told. It is the one about Snowdrop and her cruel stepmother that was so vain she must be always looking in her wonder-mirror to say: *Spieglein, Spieglein an der Wand, Wer ist die schönste im ganzen Land?* But when the little Snowdrop was grown up, the mirror must tell the truth, so it must say in answer to the Queen's question: *Frau Königin, Ihr seid die schönste hier aber Schneewittchen ist tausendmal schöner als Ihr.* So this puts the Queen in a fine fume of rage and envy. So eventually Snowdrop is cast off into the forest, with all the other little German fairystory princesses. And by and by of course the little Snowdrop grows right up and marries her prince. And the wicked stepmother? Ah well, this is what happens to her. She falls in with the happy wedding-party and they take her by force and make her dance in red-hot shoes until she is dead: *Da musste sie in die rotglühenden Schuhe treten und so lange tanzen, bis sie tot zur Erde fiel.* See the idea? Well, try it on the baby.

Oh how deeply neurotic the German people is, oh how it goes right through and isn't just the leaders, like they pretend in *The Times.* Oh they are so strained and stretched and all the time they are wanting something so yearningly, it is something they don't quite know, like a dream or something that is out of focus. Oh they are wanting it all the time and stretching out their hands, oh you feel you must cover your face, it is not decent to look at that.

It is like that Sir Phoebus that is back in Rule Britannia, with his dark face and capacity for getting bored, like he gets more bored more quickly than anyone I know, like he said about his fountain pen, that day it squirted up all over his face, and the next day it did the same, only it squirted all over my frock, and he said: Why the old pen is getting vicious in its old age, it's getting real vice into it, we shall have it peeping through a keyhole soon, peering through the keyhole at a franc a time. See.

Well I had that feeling in Germany, like the people were stripping themselves too naked, and doing it with oh such lovey-dovey yearning, yes, and saying: Is there anything more beautiful than the naked body? Oh yes thanks, right off without any call to hard work, I can think of things that are a whole lot more beautiful than the naked body.

Well this nakedness of Germany, with all its whimpering lovey dovey get-all-together, and with its Movements, and Back to Wotan, and Youth Youth Youth, it makes you feel: God send the British Admiralty and the War Office don't go shuffling on with their arms economies too long-o.

Ugh that hateful feeling I had over there, and how it was a whole race was gone run mad. Oh heaven help Deutschland when it kicks out the Jews, with their practical intelligence that might keep Germany from all that dream darkness, like the forests had got hold of them again, and the Romans calling their Legions back along the Via Aurelia.

So four days after we got set in Neuesdorf I said Good-bye to Ludmilla. There wasn't anything I could do for her; and good-bye to that kiddo, and got well away before the nasty little husband rat returned to his family. And back I went to Berlin where my Jew friends let me have the run of their house, seeing they were away on holiday in Bavaria, and hadn't got anything but a poor relation in to do the washing for them. So there I stayed, with that sweet boy Karl to take me round. But the heart had gone out of it all and Karl said he understood and I just could not bear Germany but was panting to get out.

Oh how I felt that feeling of cruelty in Germany, and the sort of vicious cruelty that isn't battlecruelty, but doing people to death in lavatories. Now how I remember how Karl said, No. This was when Karl was in England years before. No, Karl said, Germans couldn't be so cruel like they said at the beginning of the war, and after discounting for recruiting propaganda as I did, never could they be even so cruel as was left, after discounting as I said.

But oh now well, then he said, what the Russians did to the German prisoners on the

Russian front that, like that is too bad to be set down, but No, Germans could not bear to see, even to see such cruelty, they could not bear it, they would be mad.

But then see what they did this time to the Jews and the Communists, and later than this right nowadays to the Jews and the Communists, in the latrines, and the cruel beating and holding down and beating, and enjoying it for the cruelty.

Oh how deeply neurotic the German people is, and how weak, and how they are giving themselves up to this sort of cruelty and viciousness, how Hitler cleared up the vice that was so in Berlin, in every postal district some new vice, how Hitler cleared that up all. And now look how it runs with the uniforms and the swastikas. And how many uniforms, how many swastikas, how many deaths and maimings, and hateful dark cellars and lavatories. Ah how decadent, how evil is Germany to-day.

Now when a people has dictators, that is a symptom that they are running mad. They should then be watched. I think they should be watched very closely. And later they should be prevented. Now think it is not a nation but an individual, now see, this is like he had a disease.

Why see, what is the matter with that poor Mr. Brown that has been looking so funny, he certainly looks queer, he looks a sick man? Oh yes, where is that Mr. Brown that we don't see now, it is a long time, that was sick? Oh yes he was sick. Oh yes he got dictators, it turned out afterwards. That's what he got. Oh certainly he was bad, very phony very queer, but he got dictators like the doctors said. Ya, that's what he got, he been put away mister this long time now. Put away, locked up and prevented.

Now it was about this time I had lunch with Karl at the Café des Westens, and I hadn't the heart to look up. I don't rightly remember what we had to eat, it was all in a daze, and presently Karl came on to the platform to wave good-bye: Good-bye Pompey. *Komm'oubald zurück.*

I was very sad, very low in my feeling then, leaning out of the window waving good-bye to Karl, very full of a feeling of all the cruelty in the world, very full of a vision of cruelty like when I trod on that snake on the hill-top near Hythe in Kent, like always snakes give me this feeling, how I will never never go in to the snake house at the Zoo, how I went through the snake house at the Berlin Zoo with Karl with my eyes cast down, so I would not look till we came to the alligators, which animals I do not so dislike, not in the way I am disgusted at the snakes.

The train now started and I sat back in my seat, I was feeling very low, this feeling had taken hold of me in Berlin, and at Neuesdorf, to such a point that I had written to my cousin Joan, the one that is a trained nurse in

Cairo. That one is very practical very sound, there is no nonsense anywhere at all about that Joan, she is engaged. Her fiancé is an engineer. They are both out there in Egypt. Oh how sound and kind is Joan, very practical. She has all the desert and the sphinx to look at by moonlight for her engagement, and Dick her fiancé they go off to the desert sands at midnight, after their work is done they go off in the abominable car that Dick made out of bits all put together by himself, and it goes very abominable, very noisy. So they go off picnicking in the desert. And do they think it is romantic? They have never once had such a soppy thought.

Joan writes to me 'We went out last night at midnight to see the Sphinx I don't think much of it. And the Pyramids, no I don't think much of them, like all their cracked up to be. No we don't think much of them we're not partial to pyramids. We had some half cooked sausages with us that we cooked up over a fire that Dick and I built up. It was grand. We got it going fine in no time. We had some ginger beer that Dick had brought with him but it was a bit flat. How are all at home? Well no more now write soon love from Joan.'

So I wrote to Joan from Berlin. It eased that feeling I had of cruelty and strain and awful dreams that was in the air all round me, but even that didn't get rid of that feeling only put it a little way away, like it was a noise coming through the fog.

So presently the train got well started up, and I sat back and, and I felt real wicked the way I had felt about the Jews myself. As if that thought along might swell the mass of cruelty working up against them, like when I sent my poems to F. Caudle, the girl that taught me English at school, she said. She was real struck on church was this girl. And she said they were just another nail in the cross that they put the Lord on, or maybe it was just another thorn in the crown that they put on Him, but the idea was, see, they was just swelling the mass of all the evil and cruelty in the world. But I thought then, well that's not how they are at all, she certainly has got them all wrong, yes, she's just got them all wrong from beginning to end.

But when I get feeling low like this, this comes back to me, and this and all the other things I have thought bad about people, and that certainly people ought to be careful what they go saying about people's poems, and I certainly will say this about F. Caudle, there was no sense nor judgement in that remark of hers that was quite uncalled for.

And I will say: What about swelling the mass of cruelty in the world by uncalled for remarks about people's poems, eh? What about that? You certainly want to think before you go making remarks about people's poems. There certainly was a lot of upstage work about F.C., she was very superior very eclectic was F.C., she had a way of saying: We who care for the finer things of life. Like meaning *I* who care etcetera, but letting you in for pure manners' sake, and not to leave the poor dog out in the cold, pure magnanimity and not a word of honest truth in it, just wicked superiority and electicism like I said, and none of the *nihil humanum mihi alienum puto* bonhomie, like Cato certainly didn't act like he meant.

But I got back thinking how they might treat dear Rosa. And oh how I suddenly warned up to Rosa thinking of her and Herman, and yes even Lottie, yea and even I'll go further and say that husband of hers, whose name I forget, though you'll find it written if you turn back a page or two. Well I got loving these people set there in this train and thinking what the Nazis might and certainly would do to them, and to Leonie whom I truthfully like and no whittling it down, whom I certainly like, respect and admire, Leonie and her little girl. Oh how frightful if they ever got coming to Germany nowadays, which they certainly wouldn't, having that practical common sense which is so the mark of their race.

Oh I thought of this and all the wicked cruelty in the world. Then I was so unquiet and distracted I began to cry like I would never stop. I didn't feel embarrassed I thought the carriage was full of Germans, and crying doesn't matter in Germany like it does in

England, and certainly the man opposite me was looking real German, so I guessed they'd think I'd said good-bye to my boy. And why shouldn't I cry. So I cried and the tears came down my cheeks, it was certainly a flood. And presently when I wasn't any longer crying quite so much, I looked across, and there was the man opposite me going to sleep. Well, that do you think, he was going to sleep-o, just rolling his head about and tossing like he hadn't got quite off, and there on the table in front of him was lying a copy of *Lady Chatterley's Lover,* I could read the title upside down. Well and there was he going bye-bye, so I acted real quickly. I said: If you're going to sleep, would you mind if I read your book for a bit? And what do you think? He was English all the time, so he said: Yes.

So I got hold of that book and I read it hard, and I got right on with it. I'd never had the chance to read it before, though I have had a great respect for D.H. since I read his *Kangaroo,* his *Lost Girl,* his memoir of M.M. that certainly was his good one, and since I read his short story *St. Mawr and The Rocking Horse Winner.* These of his, with *The Plumed Serpent,* are the ones I like best. So now I thought I will read this one. That man opposite slept like a child, he slept like that he did, on and on.

So presently we got to dinner time. So I was the only one in that carriage that was taking dinner, so I took the book along with me. I certainly was real grateful to get the opportunity of reading this book when I had been feeling so sad, it was like a rainbow. This was before there was an edition published in England. It was the contintental edition, which I guess the sleeping nit-wit opposite me had got in Paris, thinking it was just one snap from start to finish. And I laughed to think the heavy going he'd have to make and not one little snap for him. And fifteen good Manchester—that was where he came from—shillings spent, and nothing but exasperation for it.

Well at dinner the steward put me at a table for two, well I sat there reading reading, and presently he brought up the other side of the table a man that was a man about fifty, with a pointed beard, thinking: I'm not a bad looking man, well set up and carrying my fifty years as if they were half that number. So I went on reading, reading, and he was staring at me like they had told him he certainly had got lovely magnetic eyes, like they'd all been telling him this for his years, ever since he was a little boy. It was his mother began it. So when I had put down the book to eat he said: *Sind Sie deutsch? Nein. So. Italienisch? Nein. Und so was? Leider bin ich nur englisch.* So then he leant across, very magnetic in the eyes, and said: I know everything you are thinking.

Phew-oops dearie, this was a facer, and a grand new opening gambit that I hadn't heard before. I could only think to say: Well, well, well. The dinner by this time was coming on good. I mean the soup was absolutely first rate, and afterwards there was roast duck, very good indeed. So I was beginning to feel: Well, there is nothing to be done about it, about the Jews and the atavism and the decadence, no there's nothing to be done about it. So, help yourself to another helping of apple sauce, Pompey, I said: Help yourself to a second helping of apple sauce.

So by and by I heard my friend opposite was still talking. So on he went, it was a bit difficult to follow since he wouldn't speak in German, thinking how he was *fine*, my dear boy, just *fine* at English, so on he went. Well after the roast duck we had some ice bomb pudding with hot chocolate sauce, that was very good indeed, so then we had a savoury that was angels on horseback so then we had coffee. Then I heard this boy opposite was saying: say he was saying would I go back with him to his compartment, so would I, I would not.

So then I looked at him and he seemed not hateful really, but rather sweet in a way, talking all the time and just playing up to those magnetic eyes of his he'd been told about.

So he was going to England this boy was, and trying to raise a loan in the grand old city of London, and I guessed he had not one hope of doing it. and I thought there was something sad about it all, but I know that thar grand old city of London, and how fine and quick they are at summing a boy up, and how they are being oh-so-o-charming all the time, just not a bit pompous oh dear no, not like the French and the German business men. Oh these Stock Exchange people are awfully sweet and old chappie, and underneath if you haven't got good introductions, good security, all very slap up and o.k., you might as well try and get capital out of a cow. Yes but they say No, they say No, so bright and smiling-o, so chummy and intimate, so you wouldn't think it was No, or if you did, you wouldn't think you'd got the right man. Oh no, a man that was so charming, so elegant, he could not know a thing about money, oh horrid money, oh no. It was the wrong man I saw, such a charming fellow, the son of old Lord Hoop that won the international rose tree trophy. But that was the right man, my little foreign fellow, that was the right man all right, and what he said was what he said. Was No.

So I thought of all that would be happening to this man to-morrow. So I let him down easy, I said: You know as a matter of fact I'm a bit preoccupied at the moment, so perhaps you will excuse me. He fetched a mighty sigh at this and said, yes he too was preoccupied, and didn't I say then, out it all came, about how he had to go to London to get capital, and it was all up if he didn't, and that's why there he was travelling first class and having what might likely be his last good dinner.

Oh they don't do you so badly at the Great Eastern, I said. And he smiled a sad sad wistful smile, implying how I hadn't really understood that it wasn't *just* a case of number one cook shop, but oh so much deeper than that, so too deep for words. But if there's one thing I dislike in a dinner-partner it is emotional tension. So—I let it go at this.

That was the last time I was ever abroad, and please help me that is the last time, it will remain so, so long I get this one fortnight holiday. It is too little for too much, to go abroad this way and back again so soon.

You are so tired when you come back. It is funny being like I am so tired, such a lot, it is funny, you can get a funny feeling out of it do you know. It is as if you weren't quite in focus maybe, it is like being a bit drunk, so you were lit up but still able to sit up and stand up and walk and smile, but it is there all the time, everything is shifted a bit the wrong way, like it was just a bit everything like G.K.C. says *the wrong shape*. But very funny, very funny-peculiar the whole way along.

It is funny how in that state anything might happen, and the most familiar things get a twist of the unordinary about them, like it was a dream. Oh how you pray to get the really ordinary, and the dream starts off. Well how's this, nothing to grumble about here. Why here's old Piccadilly and going along to Ridgways, and these people are just plum ordinary, *they might be real*.

They might be real. They might be real. I said they might—oh whoa up here, this is the password that lets you right in on that anarchy of dreaming sleep.

Oh there was an invalid for you—that fine writer de Quincey, that had all those purple passages I used to get by heart. That bit that I said that he said, that anarchy of dreaming sleep, well now that is a purple patch. But when you're right in the middle of this anarchy then you don't care so much about purple patches, you don't think much of them, sniff, like cousin Joan in Egypt, you just don't think much of them.

Often when I am dreaming asleep I look at myself in a mirror, and I think. Why I might be real it's so good it's just like you could touch it. And often I look at Sir Phoebus, that's the dark boy face I said, and when I am wide awake-o I look at this dark boy face over the desk and I think: Hurra, he's so damn good he might be real.

Well when you are getting so tired, or when you are getting so ill, that's the way you get.

And there's a great deal of useful observations to be made in that state, providing you go with it, you go with it like you were at the dentist, and he was giving you an anaesthetic, and he was saying: Breathe deeply. Which means to say, go with it, don't fight against it.

So you go with it this state, and very rich and very curious can that experience be. But if it is to be fully rich and curious like I said, you must have an anchorage, someone that is fine and honest and strong, as de Quincey had his sister, and I have the Lion of Hull. Oh how kind these people are, that are so kind to invalids, that don't pester them with emotional demands, that don't ever do this at all, but are there, with common sense and a jug of laudanum for Tommy, with common sense and a jug of hot milk for Pompey. These women are the salt of the earth, sisters and aunts, and some mothers are like that too, but it's more difficult if you are a mother, you have to have emotional contacts, and that can worry and pester and drive your kiddo down the steep place into the sea all right, and some aunts too are that way.

Oh how deeply thankful I am I didn't go having an aunt with clever ideas about literature and painting. Oh how I dread those cultured gentlewomen, like you get so many of in America. Oh my, they put in so much energy getting cultured it frays their nerves, they're all profoundly unquiet these women, and running out after the last opinion. Oh it is a pity such people learnt to read. They think there is credit and Society in knowing about books and pictures, so they go on knowing more and more things about them, like: This is where the painter sat, and this is where this writer had his sleep-o.

And supposing you do know about pictures and books, supposing you do know in the rich full way about them, what credit it that? No one that knows in the rich full way about pictures and books would ever think there was any credit in knowing like this. Why, such a soppy thought would never come to him. But oh you want to be careful nowadays the way you go talking about these things. You want to keep very mum-o, and you want to keep the smarties off, oh yes they can read now, and very cunning they are the way they pick things up, very quick and cunning, much fiercer about it they are than the people who do it because they like it, very much fiercer. Because they're out for social credit-marks. Oh yes they are. And there's nothing fiercer than the credit-mark hunt there certainly is not.

I don't think this feeling has been about in the air so very long, not so very long. I think it's all come with everybody learning to read, and getting it all mixed up with the social game, and the fashion papers. Like that superior fashion paper that gives nice clothes to its readers and gilt-edged ideas all ready to try on for their dinner party conversations. So that you can get a run on El Greco one year. And that's fine, that's all right. El Greco for 193-something. Who gave you El Greco for 193-something? Eh? Well you put down your name now right away for one year's subscription. We never yet let a reader down. Oh *my dear,* haven't you heard, why, she's still talking about El Greco?

It all lines up with the advertisements, those *chic* balloon conversations they have you know: My dear, how can we tell that nice Mrs. Snooks? Why she still washes her face the old way. Won't anybody tell her she'll never get a partner while she talks about El Greco?

So you see you want to be careful how you go talking about books and pictures nowadays. But that's no reason why you shouldn't look at them provided you keep it to yourself, or go with one or two picked men and true, who won't blab.

And don't go running down the safe and ordinary when you think oh, you are oh so tired of not meeting interesting people. Don't you go doing it, or one day things will get the twist for you like I was saying, and you go up to have tea with that boring old Mrs. Tombe, and you get into her sitting room and she'll have her hat on same as usual, and the blinds half down for the sake of her complexion, and it will be a big shady hat. And by and by she'll say: Two lumps Mr. Blimp or three? I always forget. And you'll look at her for the first time, and it'll just be an old parrot that's jabbering like I said, with its hat on.

And the room that you'll hang on to for *ordinariness*, having had a bit of a shock over that parrot, will go curving and swirling round and away, and presently you'll be out in the dark night nowheres that you know, nowheres that is even pretending to be ordinary.

I get the idea that that's what will happen when we're dead, dead and gone-o, and we shall spend eternity wishing we could set eyes on Aunt Martha's old fur cape, set eyes on it and not have it changing right away into the landscape we have come to hate so much. But that maybe is a pessimistic view of eternity and I don't say it's all fixed up that way at all, but I do say don't go running down the safe and ordinary. Hang on to it.

I just now went to stay with a friend of mine that got married. And when I got down there sure enough there she was married to a man that was—and after all I've said about Germany what black treachery and perfidy this is—well I'll say it, got married to a man that is a Jew, and the sort of Jew not like Herman or Bennie that has an artistic temperament working overtime on all cylinders, but just a plain ordinary safe business-man of a Jew with a whole hell of a great idea about money. Well, this girl was an intellectual sort of a girl, quiet, very quiet, and a regular dark horse. Well no doubt that's where he came in. He was a fine hearty he was, and never had no views about things that weren't cut and dried, and never had no bother thinking there might be something to be said on the other side. On no he knew and he didn't keep it to himself. Like he said: Ha ha ha, the I.W.W.

I don't rightly know what this stands for, but perhaps it is The Industrial Workers of the World, and just a bit self conscious about that all. So this husband said: Ha ha ha the I Won't Work's. That was a good one. Ever heard that before? Well, I can't say I haven't heard it before. But it was a long time ago. And anyway: please go on.

Well he had chosen a Scotch name like they do, and his brother was there, and he had chosen a Scotch name too, like they do, but they hadn't chosen the same Scotch name, that was a pity. There's no harm in Jews having Scotch names, no harm at all, but brothers should agree on the same Scotch name, or agree to compromise on a hyphen. But not a bit of it, the brother had a different Scotch name. He had neurasthenia too. It took him this way, he was always making puns, very queer and neurasthenic, every sentence had a pun in it. But he was *souffrant*, very *souffrant*, and there was something sweet about that brother. I did not so-o-o much like my friend's husband, though for her I dare say he gave her that feeling of the safe and ordinary that she was wanting. But I shouldn't know. So this brother was much more *sympatisch*. And so when he said to me, very humble very quiet: Would you sit on my knee? I did not say: I am rather preoccupied, will you excuse me if I don't? No, I did not mind if I did. So I did.

Now this brings us slap up against that mighty ogre Sex that is a worse ogre to the novelist than those family histories I so cleverly avoided a few pages back. But oh how I have enjoyed sex I do enjoy myself so much I cannot pass it over. So there I was sitting on this man's lap and thinking he was rather sad and sweet, and thinking I was stopping him having to make puns because of his neurasthenia, because if he was having me sitting on his knee he didn't have to be making puns all the time, and it was restful for everyone, even if I hadn't thought he was so sad and sweet, and a great improvement on his brother.

Some people take sex like it was a constitutional exercise, some people take it like it was a conflict. Some people have to mix it up with a lot of talk, explaining and arguing and declaiming, and some people take it like it was all hatred and cruelty.

Those are the people that have never rightly got away from *cenobites* like St. Anthony. If you can fix those people up with a girl that likes thinking she is her whole sex laid down for a sacrifice and an atonement, then fast and furious is the fun they two can have, like the poem:

Through sacrificial tears,
And anchoretic years,
  Tryst
With the sensualist

But that tryst is full of awful hazards. Yea, it certainly is long odds against you don't find no sensualist at all. And after all those years, and sick with hope deferred, it certainly takes a strong heart and high fettle not to get cynical when the girl friend turns up at last and doesn't want anything, no nothing but a home and a b-a-b-y. My heart goes out to that anchorite that waited all that time and had nothing for him at the end but discord and exasperation.

Now when I was staying with Harriet another reason why I never got early to my bed was this, that she had a boy that was always not at peace with himself, but always must be beating up trouble for himself, and no doubt that's the way he enjoyed it, but it wasn't what Harriet was looking for, though he was a sweet boy too, and she was always hoping that he'd give up his questioning, like he was no longer an undergraduate, and should have left that behind, but carried it along with him, not trailing, not like clouds of glory at all, but just plum obduracy and *jeunesse*, that he should have left behind when he turned twenty-five. And late enough then.

Now what strikes me now plum out of all this plether of words is just this: two diseases we have right here that the modern world is suffering from—*dictators* like I said and *cenobites* like I said too. A man can have cenobites like he can have dictators, and sometimes the same man can have both, which certainly is hard luck for mum and dad when the kiddo goes that way, and no wonder people aren't so keen dead struck on bringing people into the world, like they might go down with *dictators* and *cenobites* and bring misery and suffering to their loved ones.

Cenobites just can't take sex as they find it, it has to be conflict and frustration and really so-o-o important in a way it isn't really at all important, though it is important in the way if it wasn't there it would be a pretty punk world. But you could never say of a cenobite that he enjoyed sex, no you couldn't hardly say that, not that he enjoyed sex, oh no not to say enjoy. Sometimes, funny how it is, you get a cenobite that genuinely feels he ought to enjoy sex, and he goes all out panting and straining, he goes all out to enjoy sex, but of course never does he get anywhere near enjoying it at all, because Venus isn't to be caught, not to be caught in that net. Oh no, Venus goes off laughing up her sleeve, and leaving torments behind for the fool, because although she laughs up her sleeve, she don't like it, no she won't stand for that sort of thing, so off she goes, laughing that nasty cynical laugh that echoed through the vales of Thessaly, leaving torments and tribulations for the fool that had offended her.

For they offended her in those days too but not in the same undergraduateish way they do nowadays. But the torments and the Mrs.

Haliburton's troubles they get is much the same. *Vénus toute entière à sa proie attachée.* Sometimes she will just plum tear the living heart out of him, but mostly she goes off laughing, leaving the stings and the scorpions behind for the fool. There's nothing Venus hates more than a fool. Now boys, three cheers for Venus, hip hip hip hurray.

Oh how I enjoy sex and oh how I enjoy it. There have been many funny things about sex in my life that have made me laugh and so now I will tell you.

There was once a woman called Miss Hogmanimy. That was certainly a queer name. That was a name you would certainly want to get married out of. But this woman was very queer and wrought up over babies and the way babies are born, and she gave up her whole life going round giving free lectures on how babies are born. And it certainly was queer how ecstatic she got about this way how babies are born, and always she was giving lectures to young girls of school or school-leaving age. And all the time it was mixed up in a way I don't just remember with not drinking, not drinking alcohol, but just carrying on on ginger beer, kola and popgass. And so well this Miss Hogmanimy she got up in our school, now I think it was our school, chapel and so there she was in this school chapel, giving a lecture with illustrating slides to young girls on how babies are born.

Well my aunt didn't rightly hold with this Miss Hogmanimy for she thought, that's my aunt did, that there wasn't no mystery about the way babies was born, but simple and straightforward, and much the same all times, barring local differences and complications, like you had to have the doctor for, Miss Hogmanimy or no Miss Hogmanimy.

But to listen to Miss Hogmanimy you'd think just knowing straight out how babies was born was to solve all the problems of adolescence right off. You'd come out straight and simple and full of hearty fellowship and right thinking if you just got it clear once and for all how babies are born. There'd be no more coming out in spots and getting self-conscious about the senior prefect, nor getting a crush on the English mistress, nor feeling proud and miserable like you do at that time, before you get grown up. There'd be none of this at all if you just knew how babies are born. So there she was.

And somehow my aunt was overprevailed upon and there was me too and my school friend. At that time we were both of us working for matriculation, but were out to learn. We didn't mind if we did you know, with an eye open for the facts of the case.

And what did we get? First of all Miss Hogmanimy got a special way of speaking like losing her puff a bit in an uphill climb, it was very like this a sort of breathless whisper that could yet be heard, I'll say that for her, she could be heard. But oh what nonsense she had to say, and how foiled we felt, my friend and I, because all she said was always saying: Oh how beautiful it all is, and how it is the holiest thing on earth, and she would pray a prayer first of all, and we waited and waited, and hoped some time we would get the facts, but no it was all this funny breathless whisper.

Well the upshot of it all was she wanted us to sign a paper saying we would never drink anything but ginger beer and allied liquids. And she had a smile that was very cunning and deliberate. It came out like it was spontaneous, but somehow you knew it was so-o-o spontaneous, but cleverly timed. Very cunning and clever was this smile, and she said: Now girls if you are at a dinner and they offer you wine, don't make a fuss, we needn't make a fuss, but just say: I don't take that, thank you. But you would somehow give the impression that what you thought about the person that offered you wine was, that that person was right up to the neck in moral turpitude.

And of course round about here Miss Hogmanimy would enlarge upon how alcohol leads to irregularity in sexual behaviour. Oh what a lovely phrase that is, and how it does *not* describe the way you feel at parties sometimes, if you have your right friends there, and that lovely feeling, you get quite shot up, and it is lovely oh how I enjoy it.

But of course about this I did not learn until long after the day of Miss Hogmanimy.

But right at this time at school I was studying Greek for matriculation and the play, we were learning to act it in Greek, as we did always once a year, was the *Bacchae* of Euripides. Our classics mistress was dead shot on Euripides though I can't altogether agree with her. For instance he is rather a shadow I think, a dark shadow of emotion, to throw into hard relief the bright lovely hard and religious formalism of the representative Greeks. Why Racine I think is more Greek than Euripides. But here now I will say I cannot read Greek now, I have almost forgotten everything except by heart the part I had to learn, which I can still say after all these years, though I cannot tell you what it means word by word, but can only give you a précis of it, can only give you The Story of the Speech. It is the speech of the second messenger, very long, very long, over a hundred lines, got by heart with some difficulty, but got by heart and remembered now.

But this emotionalism and soft feeling for the social inferiority of women, which almost brings you slap up against Miss C. Pankhurst, and the rights of the individual, and the human heart afraid and torn apart by its own conflicting emotions, no no—that is not the Greek pattern at all.

But even here my thoughts of Euripides are coloured by the still more too human translator he has now in England, for whom our classics mistress had also a very deep, very human feeling, very soft and penetrating. Ah all *too* human. That spoils it all. It is utterly hateful. It is this. He is translating Medea. Medea has heard that Jason wishes to make a marriage of convenience, to ally himself with the reigning house of Corinth. Medea says, and he translates it so:

O Zeus, O Earth, O Light,
Will the fire not stab my brain?
What profiteth living? Oh,
Shall I not lift the slow,
Yoke, and let Life go,
As a beast out in the night,
To lie, and be rid of pain?

Now there is no mention in the Greek of any beast or any night, there is no mention of this at all, that is just an imaginative, a too human soft imaginative rendering of the original Greek. But look again at the Greek, what is there is 'bad enough'. I put that in inverted commas because I mean *bad enough* in the sense that I am saying, not Greek but Barbarian in its soft human feeling, very barbarian, very emotional.

But, you will say, Medea was a barbarian. That is absolutely nothing. It does not count at all that she was a barbarian. The Greek pattern cannot be upset because some barbarian has his feelings lacerated, and goes to tell everybody about the lacerations he has. No that is not at all permissible. So in the Greek you have 'O Zeus, O Earth, O Light'—that is all right, that is a formal invocation. That passes. Then there is an appeal to the thunderbolts of heaven to destroy her, to strike her down. That is there. Then there is the thought: What further use is life to me? Then there is the thought: How pleasant it would be to die, to lay down this hateful life in death.

Well that is rather emotional, yes. But this professor he makes it still more emotional, so that altogether it is hateful and not Greek at all. It is a pity this professor makes bad worse. I must not run on here, but I do not like this, I do not like this riot of emotion, I do not like it at all.

Well see, now look at Racine, and see what I am saying. Look at Euripides' *Hippolytus,* and now look at Racine's *Phèdre*. It is the same story, the same story altogether, but Euripides is very profoundly unquiet and restless, so that it disturbs the tragedy, but Racine is very serene, very severe, very austere and simple, and the tragedy very strong and not broken up at all, but very strong and simple. And this tragedy is also very bracing, and whereas with the other you feel ashamed and draw aside, with a *noli-me-tangere* withdrawal of the skirts, here it is very strong and very inevitable and impersonal. This is Greek. This is truly Greek, and what the Greek is.

Now the story of *Phèdre* is very well known, but perhaps the story of the *Bacchae* is not so well known. But it is a story that I shall now tell you, and you will think it is not suitable for children. And no perhaps it is not very suitable for children, if you have that point of view about children. But this is a far better play than *Medea*, so now I will tell you.

It is about Dionysus, and there is a lot of Dionysus-magic in this play, that is a little bit frightening perhaps. Dionysus has no good feelings, no not one, he has no good feelings and no high sentiment, he is very cynical and laughs a lot, very cruel and very cynical. So he is the son of Zeus and Semele. And Pentheus is ruler of this Theban land. And Pentheus is the nephew of Semele that died, that was burnt up in a great flame, that died, and had her grave with the sacred fire burning on it always, that died, and Dionysus lived, and was taken by Zeus and held by Zeus in his thigh, till Dionysus was old enough to go about by himself.

So now Pentheus is living in the royal palace, and he has there with him his mother Agave, and other women of the Court. And no, Pentheus is very stubborn, rather stupid very stubborn. No, he will not recognize the divinity of Dionysus. He had played with Semele as a child. No, Semele never had a divine son. No aunt ever had a divine son, so he would not worship Dionysus. But the women and Agave they had feelings of forebodings about this sturdy attitude of Pentheus, they thought no good would come of it.

So presently Dionysus heard, and laughed and laughed, and came down to Thebes laughing and swift, and very divine and furious. And he was disguised. And he now drove the women mad, they were all driven mad, they ran to the mountains with the divine frenzy of madness upon them, and they ran and ran, leaving their husbands and their children. Up on the wild mountains they ran, and they had their thyrses, and there they were run mad on the wild mountains worshipping Dionysus, and so strong in their madness they would pick up wolf cubs, and hold them up and give them the milk that their children should have had, and they would laugh and laugh and hunt the lion, and capture him, and with their naked hands pull him to pieces, tear him, tear his head off, pull him entirely to pieces, they were so mad and so powerful in their madness. There were no women left in Thebes at all.

Now very softly and quietly, very deceitfully in the hot afternoon, Dionysus comes into the palace, the palace is very quiet and empty, he comes into the palace, nobody challenges him, he is laughing softly all the time. So he comes to the King, and he tells the King: Why is it Pentheus, where are all the women? But Dionysus is disguised, and the King is so sad because the women are all run mad, he does not think: I am a King, why should this curious-looking man question me? There is something about him I do not like. I do not trust him. Why should this man question me?

No, he talks with Dionysus always disguised, and laughing very softly to himself: Why Pentheus do you not follow the women and bring them back? Why *Pentheus*, the strong plain blunt straightforward man, so honest, with no nonsense, why nobody could get round you? Why, surely, surely you will follow the women, and bring them back? Why, it would be funny if you did anything else but follow the women and bring them back. Why, people would certainly laugh. Why, if I said: Why, Pentheus will not follow the women, he will let them go, he will let them go run mad. Why, at first they would not believe me. But we know Pentheus he is just a plain honest man, he is not that sort of man, it must be somebody else. But then so later they would believe me, and then they would believe me, and they would laugh, and presently the laughter would be very loud, and it would be very loud and it would last a very long time. And you would go into your palace. But no, the laughter would be there too, very loud, very clear. So you would go into your bedchamber, but at once you would see that it was impossible to go into your bedchamber, at once you would see that the bedchamber was full of the laughter, that it was there that the laughter was all the time: Well here it is, how foolish, and not outside at all as I thought.

So now Dionysus began to laugh out loud. At first he began to laugh very softly out loud, but then not so softly, and then very loudly, and then Pentheus began to laugh too: 'Why did I distrust this man?' He thinks: 'he is very funny, he has made me laugh, so now it is weeks since I have laughed.'

So later they are getting on finely together. And then Dionysus learns that Pentheus is afraid to go near the women, because they are god-driven-mad, and can tear lions apart, and will allow no man to go near them. No man is to go on that mountain, they will tear him apart like a lion.

So Dionysus says very softly, very winning and casual: But Pentheus my dear fellow, that's easy, dress up as a woman. Now there is something dishonourable for a King to dress up as a woman, but there is something no longer honourable at all in Pentheus, he is sniggering and laughing all the time, he no longer has any dignity, or any honour. So this is a fine idea his new friend had. So they laugh and laugh, and get women's clothes, and Dionysus drapes them round Pentheus: *My dear,* how do you like this peplum, do you think it goes? This fold looks better hanging so; don't you think? He makes the King turn and walk and turn, he is very difficult to satisfy is Dionysus. But at last every fold is in place, and the head gear is just right, and he gives him the thyrsis: My dear chap you look just like a rather serious-minded slightly pompous female, just like my old aunt I'll tell you about next time. My dear, nobody would think you weren't at least a woman and perhaps an aunt and mother. Oh I think we'll let you keep your own sandals. *It's a pretty stiff climb up those mountains.*

So now Pentheus feels a little cold, as if he were caught in a swift current. So now he is beginning to feel he has to go up to that mountain and see those women, but it is a force coming from outside makes him have to, have to go.

So now Dionysus takes him by the arm, propelling him, very friendly very strong. Dionysus leads him, pushes him outside of the palace, and the current is getting swifter, and Pentheus doesn't even care so much about it now, he will just go, it doesn't matter much, his nice friend says to go, he's a jolly good fellow this friend, with heaps of funny ideas. So Pentheus goes along laughing, and laughing goes along out of the town, and up the path, getting narrower and steeper, and laughing softly to himself. And at the bend going out of sight he thinks he ought to have looked behind before, it's a bit ungrateful, with this nice friend of his helping him with all those funny ideas, it doesn't look a generous act at all to go straight on like he was, without ever turning to wave to that nice new friend of his. So he gets to the bend and looks down.

There is Dionysus looking taller and bigger, and different. And laughing. Like it wasn't so much a laugh, as something he can't put a name to, not so much a laugh, but it is a laugh, but a grin, something like he'd seen before, with all those teeth. Ha ha, he was just pulling a funny face, that was all, he certainly was a boy with funny ideas, it was nothing at all of course about his being bigger, it was just a trick of the distance. So: Goodbye, shouts Pentheus: Goodbye, and thanks a lot. And: Goodbye, shouts Dionysus: Goodbye Pentheus, give my love to Agave.

And Pentheus is never seen again alive.

This play that we did at school, with the professor I was saying about there himself, very approving and following on the script, made a very great impression on me, and I used to watch the scene in the palace where Dionysus is dressing up the King in women's clothes, and I used to laugh too, and laugh, and I used to think: Dionysus is wonderful.

But the part I was going to tell you just in the one particular speech I had to say, and how it was so incongruous, and yet how very funny, taken in line with Miss Hogmanimy and her opinions on the effect of alcohol on sexual behaviour, was just this. The last four lines of my speech, there were four of them in the Greek, and they went like this and meant just this, that I always wanted to get up and shout at Miss Hogmanimy because it was what she was saying, what she could not avoid saying, with all the weight of Education behind them. The words were, these were the words: Take away wine and there is no Cyprian, No other joy, nothing left to man.

Three cheers for Euripides and Miss Hogmanimy.

Well, chaps, I may have been a bit sketchy on the language side but from my study of the classics certainly I early got an idea of the Olympians as very beautiful, very lovely, cynical and always laughing. And very cruel, cruel in a cold callous and divine way, not with the cruelty of human beings which is of course much crueller. Because human beings can calculate to the last inch just where it is painful and how much, but the gods and goddesses and that sort of creation really can't be bothered with those ingenuities of cruelty, they just have an idea of what is due to them from mortals, and hand out penalties if they don't get it, without bothering much about the reaction of the victim. Very cruel, very callous, we think the Olympians, but of course it is hardly their fault. They have no heart. They have no heart.

Not so Miss Hogmanimy. With her bright smile, her highly polished face, her smile, her shining bright eyes, her unfashionable hat and unprovocative blouse, her clumsy hands which were for ever knocking the knobs of the rostrum, she evinced every symptom of heart possession did Miss H. But she was severe too. Hearts must go the right way. Hearts were no excuse for irregular sexual behaviour, and babies were lovely when they were legitimate. But the important thing was to get it dead right from the start the way how they were born. Legitimate or illegitimate, they all came into the world by the same painful road.

But being all tied up with love and religious sentiment, it was just impossible for her to get the medical side of the question across; she would draw sections on the blackboard and then stand her stout body in front of it, blushing furiously, it was all so holy, and all so terrible if it wasn't legitimate. And she did so hope that we would not drink wine, and that we would not wear provocative décolleté.

Looking back now I have a soft feeling for Miss Hogmanimy, her heart was in the right place but her wits were fuddled. I came away from those lectures with a profound aversion from the subject and a vaguely sick feeling when I heard of friends and relations about to produce offspring. I used to pray for them and wash my hands of it.

Very different indeed was the simple blushing idiotically ecstatic attitude of Miss H. from the blustering hearty attitude of Mr. Bosch and Miss Clytie Fennimore and the free and easy school. Mr. Bosch is always giving lectures. He was always making jokes at these lectures and is very ha-ha and always using the good old Anglo-Saxon terms. He loves to bring out those bluff old monosyllables racy of the soil, of the soil that packs the window boxes of London, W.C.1.

But obviously you can't be so-o-o free and easy unless you are prepared as a point of honour to stand by with slap-up abortion service free for the asking. Oh no, otherwise it won't do at all. The woman that embraces the sexual philosophy of Mr. Bosch is going to stake all on contraceptives. And count up the number of your married friends who have had *accidents*, little Jacks and Jills that have had to be fed and educated, and then see what sort of a stake this is.

Mr. Bosch is in favor of constitutional pressure being brought to bear on the legal pundits. But meanwhile the motto of the free and easy school is: Carry on as before. Carry on old girl, carry on, it's all such fun and the risk is really negligible, you shouldn't let yourself think so much about it, it is hampering and definitely morbid, and it's your risk anyway. Abortion? *My dear*, don't get that way. Damn it all of course not, it's a criminal offence; no I wouldn't touch it, besides it's all against my principles, it's definitely vicious, babies are good for women, it completes them you know. Food, education? Don't be such a snob—what are the board schools for? And food—nobody starves to-day. And anyway why bother about it it's one chance in a thousand. You think too much, that's what's the matter with you, you positively brood, you want to cultivate a lighter touch. It's just a glorious joke. Copulation's first class fun. Why you ought to think yourself lucky getting the chance, look at all the depressed females that never got asked, going round reeking with their unholy continence. Aw, come on, that's the baby, help me off with my wooden leg and hop into bed. Why this is fine for you, you certainly are a lucky girl.

So a little while ago they published those statistics. You know how heady it is reading those statistics. Well these statistics said how prostitution in England was definitely on the downward grade, you could hardly see an honest whore from one side of Leicester Square to the other, and as for that arcade—practically empty, my dear chap, nothing absolutely nothing but a couple of police women and an old girl up for a day's shopping on a cheap return.

Well well well, the people who do not believe in free-and-easy-does-it have no reason to congratulate themselves in this. Statistics are so misleading. Won't anyone tell them how it is, and how the free and easy school, that won't touch abortion and has such a profound dislike of *quod* pro quo, has made a blackleg of many a bright young girl that took an earnest view of her love life.

Well now there was Cynthia. Cynthia was a fine girl, an old-school-tie acquaintance of mine, and into the bargain, a social worker. To look at she was pleasant enough, though no chocolate box lovely, oh no she was yellow haired and freckled, with large green eyes and a slightly unaryan slant to her face, it was looking a bit like an egg, and the eyes set flat above broad acres of cheek bones, a bit of the peasant type, Slav for preference, you might have viewed her as Olga on the Volga. She had a plump little body and an amiable disposition. Very kind, very practical too, was Cynthia.

So later on she wasn't going to be *intacta* any longer, she was just going to develop her love life was Cynthia. So by and by she became extremely versatile, and if it wasn't Bill it was George or Brian or Barry or there was and Everard too. All these enterprising young men were in on a good thing, yes they not only got a Miss Bedworthy, they got a cookie and a char and a housekeeper and a sewing woman and everything for just asking.

So I used to think Cynthia was going blackleg all at once on a good many professions, wife, mistress and all the others like I said. She is now still going on going the same way, but I got the idea when last I saw her that it was all losing its pristine charm, just much the same as a handshake and pretty monotonous at that, so she was wishing she could round it all up with a baby, but that of course would put her right with the theorists but wrong with the authorities, and in this world of compromise you just can't let your right hand know what your left hand does.

So she was real set on social work, and very good at it all, drilling little brattos in the S.E.25, and very highly thought of and a great deal more humanly experienced than most of her official profession I'll allow. And now there she goes on throwing her heart into the brattos and trailing them round out of office hours and taking them places like the Jubilee and Kew Gardens and the Tower, and giving them parties and just keeping on. And at the moment I don't think there is a Tom, Dick or a Harry about, but that's just chance and a thing that might happen to any of us.

And there's no moral to this tale at all, but just a few remarks the censorious might make on the subject of blacklegging and the ruination by pampering of Tom, Dick and Harry, Brian, Bill and Barry for it certainly is just fine and dandy for them. But there you are with a large-hearted girl like Cynthia it's just not possible to give too much, and if you are made that way you are made that way, and all the horrid girls that bother a chap about abortion facilities or wedding rings are just not made that way. So there you are.

Did you ever see a play called Maya that's the play they always put on at the Repertory Theatre when the programme's running thin. I said, *Maya*. A very powerful piece of work and as the critics always say: A careful handling of an unpleasant theme. With the Rep. Theatre packed to the ceiling with all those many people who are genuinely interested in the careful handling of unpleasant themes, and with a red lamp hanging left side of the stage to give the more knowing a genuine hint as broad as it's long of what about that unpleasant theme, up goes the curtain and there you are, sociological ladies and gentlemen, there you are slap up in a stew in Marseilles. In and out of the stews, Stews I have Known, that's the idea, see?

But this stew is a very high toned establishment, oh very high toned indeed. There is the girl set in her apartment, it might be in an apartment block in London or New York, except for the seafaring men of rough appearance who drop in from time to time, with no other idea for all you can see but to pass the time of day having a good old chat about home life and the kids, and how are you keeping after all these months. Just dropped in to have a chat with a girl that's got a head on her shoulders and is a damned good listener too, and makes a man feel there's something in life after all, and not just sex appeal and sex appeal till the cows come home.

Very deep they used to get in their talk sometimes. There was one of these callers that had a line on Yogi, and the girl was very interested in Yogi. Before long you felt there would not be much she didn't know about Yogi. And I definitely got the idea that it was all absolutely above board and no irregular behaviour at all, but just friendly frank talks like they have Sunday afternoons at the Nudist Society, just frank talks and everybody feeling better for having got it off his chest.

And the only thing that suggested it wasn't a flat in Bloomsbury, or Greenwich Village, was the funny clothes they were wearing, like Maya herself, like they called the girl, being very deep and symbolic and linked up I make no bones with the goddess of plenty, seen through the eyes of an earnest student of anthropology and comparative religion. This Maya certainly wore clothes like she might be a prostitute, being mostly clad in wraps and kimonos and mules.

But what I say is, and this goes for the visitors that were wearing sailors' clothes most of the time, the overwhelming sense of high thinking and unplumbed respectability there was about those people just set the clothes off to count for nothing. They were just all of them nice-minded well-brought-up girls and boys, with a funny liking for fancy dress, that was a little bit boheem, but harmless, on my dear harmless. And not one of them was cynical or frivolous like some I could name, but really high minded, and always knowing that we're all of us here for the great purpose of leaving it better when we're gone. See?

And need I say there was the bit about how Maya was supporting in affable circumstances a daughter that was a regular church goer, and simply had no idea that mother was—well you know how uncharitable some people are. And she just wouldn't see her daughter though busting with natural affection yes, no, she wouldn't even see the girl, or let her come round in case she might get thinking kimonos was regulation daytime wear outside of stews.

Very affecting that bit was, and everybody came away feeling the whore's life was just one long trail of service and sacrifice, like they say about hospital nurses. And off they went home feeling real good, as if they had been to church.

I think the two subjects about which there is most nonsense talked are sex, and how to bring up children.

So now shall we talk about how to bring up children? That is an interesting subject to talk about. So now shall we talk about that, how to bring up children? Shall we talk about that, and see truth together, Mr., Mrs. or Miss Gigadibs?

My fiancé and I, did I say that my fiancé Freddy and I both live at Bottle Green? This is a healthy residential district to the north of London. None of your Hampsteads or Highgates or Golders Greens, but just straight north in a line with Enfield, which is where they make small arms and have a market place and a residential district even superior to Bottle Green.

The social round in England is very complicated, very intricate, but it is always the same in this way. Everybody is always trying to be the next step up, and that is all very hearty and makes for the survival of the *status quo.* Because, given a slight increase in income and ordinary luck, and a wife that is quick at noticing, there you are, you'll be one step up as soon as sneeze. And why destroy the social order when it affords you that fine opportunity? Why indeed? So we shall never get a revolution in *Eng.*, so long as people go on healthily envying and emulating the next step up, like I said. Oh how splendid this all is—no horrid gulf yawning between the proletariat and the next of rank.

Now Freddy certainly knows a whole lot about the people of Bottle Green, and he is a very keen observer is Freddy, and tells me a lot that is so vivid, that I might have known it myself.

But I do not know it myself, because I have never played tennis. That is important. And I have not joined an amateur dramatic club. That is also so important. That is where you meet people, as they say in our correspondence columns to all the girls who don't have young men, or can't meet young men, or can't. Well that is how it goes, they get real miserable and sad because they don't meet young men. So we say: Join a Tennis Club.

So they do, so Freddy says they do, and it is funny like hell the way they do.

This is no mistake. There was a girl that wrote to . . . Well it was one paper, no I will not say which. And this girl said she had seen a young man at the tennis club she had joined so as not to feel lonely, and so as to get fixed up with a young man, and a house or a flat and a baby. And so this young man, he would do, he was all right. And so how was she to make him propose. Just that you see, they had not spoken, but how was she to make him propose? So the Answers to Correspondents came pat: and this answer was: Arrange to play the last set with him, and then linger hopefully and perhaps he will see you home.

Oh how that is a lovely phrase. Oh how I could not have thought of that phrase it is so rich and full and so pictorial in quality. Well see, can you not see up and down the suburbs, up and down the provincial towns, up and down the country house parties, up and down India, up and down Singapore and Shanghai, how there are girls who have arranged to play the last set and who are lingering hopefully?

I do not think it is at all good advice. No. Well look; there is Mariana in the Moated Grange; there is also that White Girl that Whistler painted, very wan she is now. She is lingering now, but not hopefully, I think that one is lingering now like they say, the relatives say, of someone who is very sick—She is lingering. And it is death that is going to come up out of that mirror, and I think she will be glad, and I think we shall be glad too, when death comes up out of that mirror, so that she does not have to linger any more.

This reminds me of another picture where the girl would not linger, but would not be alone either, she was like the other girls I was talking about, she was Cynthia or Maya. Well there is this picture, it is a fine canvas, there it is oblong, well the colouring is dark, it is a dark interior with the furniture, it is Victorian very Victorian furniture, it is all very sordid, very dim. There is on the left a sofa covered in horsehair going away in perspective from the onlooker. On this sofa there is a naked girl, she is lying there. There is a fire full-centre in the hearth that catches her skin and lights it up. It is all otherwise very sombre, very full of the smell of fustian and over-crowding and close close air. Then against the mantelpiece there is leaning a man, he is fully dressed, he is a man who has a top hat on, it is slightly raked over one eyebrow, he is standing there looking down at the girl, looking down rather bored, oh yes he is looking rather bored, one leg is crossed over the other, they are both probably rather bored. Yes of course it is a Sickert, a regular little Sickert. Well perhaps it is called *Home Chat*, I forget.

But now I must come back to the subject of

Bottle Green. It is rather fascinating this subject. Yes it is rather fascinating this Bottle Green where I live, and where Freddy knows about the people. They have an idea you know, the unmarried girls have an idea, that if only they were married it would be all right, and the married women think, Well now I am married, so it *is* all right: Sometimes too of course it is all right, but sometimes they have to work very hard saying all the time: So now I am married, so now it is all right, so Miss So-and-So is not married, so that is not all right. So what.

And the girls who are not married are often getting quite desperate oh yes they are becoming quite desperate, they are saying all the time, it is like the refrain in *The Three Sisters*. It is the *leitmotiv* of all their lives. It is their *Moscow*. Marriage is to them: Oh if we could only get to *Moscow*. Oh if we could only have got to *Moscow*. By this time it would now already have been all all right.

Oh the sobs and tears and stretching and straining and contriving, and meanwhile the tennis club secretaries have every reason to be pleased, because there is at least always a sub-stratum of subscriptions which are not outstanding, because these silly fatheads will never let their subscriptions get in arrears, oh no, their subscriptions will let them in to *Russia*. At the least it will let them in to the Russia of their matrimonial ambition. Over the frontier at least, if not actually into the suburbs and citadel of *Moscow*.

From this matrimony of their dreams automatically flow all blessings and benefits. It is for them the *fons et origo*. There is nothing like it. Oh no, dear Reader, there never was anything like the idea these funny asses have of matrimony. And if unfortunately they do pull it off, how unhappy is the situation of the young man who becomes their husband, for sure enough they will very soon discover that marriage is not that *fons et origo*. And then sure enough instead of readjusting their pop-eyed dreams, instead of coming into line with reality, sure enough they will go, they will run mad, but not so excitingly and refreshingly mad as the women of Thebes, they will run mad at their husbands.

But it is their own fault. They ought to be drowned, they are so silly and make so much lamentation, and are wet, and are a burden. And are the public on whom we rely to buy and read our two-penny weeklies. And they do, they do. And that, Sir, is why we are able to pay a 15 per cent dividend on our ordinary shares and 10 per cent on the 2nd prefs. But you are too late too late at this time to try and get in on a good thing, because we are not selling, no we are holding on. And the only good thing these female half-wits ever did was to buy our publications and swell our dividends.

God loves a cheerful buyer of twopenny

weeklies, and so do we. These are the girls who believe everything our contributors tell them. They put a spot of scent behind the ear, they encourage their young men to talk about football, they are Good Listeners, they are Good Pals, they are Feminine, they Let him Know they Sew their own Frocks, they sometimes even go so far as to Pay Attention to Personal Hygiene.

It is awfully funny I think the way their allowance of fiction is doled out to these little sweeties. Because they are allowed fiction as well as instructive articles on erotics, oh yes, as well as hard hard lessons in sex appeal, they are allowed to fill their little permanently waved heads with lovely lovely dreams of the never was. That I fear is where they get their funny thoughts on matrimony.

First of all there is Fiction for the Married Woman. This is how it goes. Sure enough Miss Snooks has got married to that nice solid young fellow. But somehow the gilt is off the gingerbread. It is all washing up and peeling potatoes, and there are several *kiddies,* and the furniture isn't paid for, and is already beginning to look like it was time for some more. And oh how dim drab and dreary is life in terms of squawling brats and cash instalments. But publishers are a bit timid about that thought, because it's a bit dangerous to get in that idea about the instalment system, because, well, advertisers are so. Well let's not dwell on that horrid horrid subject. There's just one word that covers that, and that is *delete.*

So by and by an old office friend . . . Oh isn't this hateful? Oh already I am beginning to feel sick, but oh what a hateful stink. So the old friend that was there in that office, she is well dressed and has a permanent wave that looks. That looks. So this old friend she says. She says. And she sees.

She sees every grease spot, every torn trashy curtain, every slobber on Tommy's face, everything that was cheap and brightly gimcrack to begin with, already now so cheap and dull and gimcrack, and not with the lovely deep rich olive green and brown and yellow sordidity of Sickert's London interiors, but oh so full of daylight that shows, oh how it shows and shows, and is so showing all the time. And drawers and cupboards are still perhaps brightly surfaced, but handles are already since a long time off, and drawers won't shut, and the cheap labour-saving devices won't work, and the little bright twopenny clockword toy that is what Everygirl saw through this wedding ring, oh it is now all looking oh.

And the windows are not high enough to jump out of. Oh no, if it was a New York apartment, with luck you could jump right out and off away into nobility and solitude and eternity. But no no here, oh the windows don't open any longer, the drawers don't shut, the cupboard doors don't shut, the electric iron doesn't work, the refrigerator doesn't freeze, there is no silence, no solitude, no darkness, no nobility.

So into this bright little tight little hell-box comes this friend from the office, and she says and says: Why not go back to the office? The Boss is willing. There is Money there. And so the wife thinks, and by and by she says: Yes, she will come back. And then, just as she is trying to open the front door, that is in a jam, that is always in a tight set jam, Tommy knocks the stewpan over, the stewpan that had supper in it for the husband, the stewpan is very hot, and Tommy is very hurt, so the wife thinks: I very nearly left my lovely Home, my lovely Tommy, my lovely husband. But am I not married, and if you are married *it must be all right*. The friend from the office is not married, so of course she is jealous, but.

And so thinking how everything is all right because she is married, and how she must not be anything but very gentle and kind to the poor friend who is still not having any man to wash up for, but is still awfully inferior and unmarried, she must be very tactful and kind to this friend, and not, oh no, she must not say one word to make worse for this friend the awful burden of inferiority, how her arms are empty, and she has no *kiddy*. And how now she remembers the wistful look the friend had when she was bathing Tommy. When she had. When. Oh, so now you see how these stories are going do you not, they are a little bit, they make you feel a little bit . . . ?

No, that is the end, that is absolutely already much too much. You can pay too much for a good dividend.

I cannot tell you about the stories for unmarried girls, the ones that are so cleverly and coyly oh. And they are so bright and smiling, and full of pretty ideas that are all the time leading up to washing-up. You will know how they go but I cannot tell you. I am already feeling: No, I should not have said all this. It is the ugliest thing that could ever have been conceived, because it is also so trivial, so full of the negation of human intelligence, that should be so quick and so swift and so glancing, and so proud. And you Reader, whom I have held by the wrist and forced to listen, I am full of regret for you, because I have forced you to listen to this.

So I will say this at once, it is a wise thing that every intelligent, sensitive child should early be accustomed to the thought of death by suicide. This follows inevitably from what I have been saying. But do not strain or pull away, because now we are coming to that rich and spacious thought where human pride is paramount.

I will not tell you how this thought came to me when I was eight years old. When I was eight years old I went away from my parents to a convalescent home, where I was so proud and so furious to be separated from my mother

I would not eat, and I would not stop crying, I thought: If I go on crying long enough I shall die. But after crying days and days I was still alive, so then I at once became rather cynical. I thought: I am still alive after all these tears, I am still alive.

So I made other discoveries, too. There was a maid there that took a fancy to me. She used to sit me on her knee. If I was in the mood for it I could play up to her fancy, but even while I was doing this I was immensely terrified. Her feeling for me, I felt this very keenly but could not for some time understand why it so much dismayed me, was in outward appearance, so far as being hugged and set on her knee, was what in outward appearance my mother . . . ? No, do you see, but it was profoundly disturbing, how in essence her feeling was so arbitrary, so superficial, so fortuitous. And so this feeling she had for me, which was not at all a deep feeling, but as one might a pet, pat and cuddle a puppy, filled me with the fear that a child has in the face of cruelty. It was so insecure, so without depth or significance. It was so similar in outward form, and so asunder and apart, so deceitful and so barbarous in significance. It very profoundly disturbed and dismayed and terrified me.

It was a little early perhaps you see, to encounter the deceitfulness of outward similarity, and that perhaps is why this maid, who was so thoughtlessly and you would think harmlessly affectionate, terrified me first in such a way that I had never before been terrified, and touching my pride, sent my thoughts again towards death.

And the thought of death, and I understood it so far that it is possible to die by falling off a high cliff, or out of a high window, the thought of this death was very consoling and very comforting to me. It was also a great source of strength, so that I came out of that experience very strong and very proud. And the nurses and the matron who were wondering if perhaps they should not have to send me home, because though I had not as I foolishly at first thought been killing myself by crying and not eating, I was always if I did eat very easily making myself sick after eating, and making myself ill, so they thought perhaps I should go home and make room for some other child who would be made better, and not worse, by the convalescent home. Suddenly they said how sensible I was. And so I stayed on at that home a long time, and eventually came home ready to go to school, and begin the school life at nine years old.

But the fear that I had had at this convalescent home, in this way that I have told you, never left me completely, only when I was home again it transferred itself to my mother. I was afraid, not of her of course, but for her. She was very ill indeed, she was very ill, and very weak and powerless, and she had heart disease. But there was the lion my aunt who was very strong, and also my mother was very strong in her mind and character, but often I should be afraid for her.

For instance if I was out with my mother and we had to go on a tram, perhaps if there were many people, or if it was full and we had to go on top, I was afraid for her, and very furious and fierce if the tram shook at all. They shake so much they are like the Mappin terraces on a high sea. And there was my mother, and I hated the tram for her, and all the other people, it was more than I could bear with equanimity, to be so furious and so powerless. It is, yes, that is a very hateful combination, fury and impotence, and no doubt I made my mother's heart weakness much worse by being so furious, but it was almost more than I could bear without bursting.

And sometimes my mother would have the heart attack of suffocation, and again there is nothing to do for people. Then she had some medicine the doctor had given her. It had ether in it. I could give her that. But one day when I came home from school it happened she was alone in the house. I rang the bell, we had no maid, and I waited, and then at last she came and let me in, and I saw that she was having a heart attack.

First of all I could not do anything for her. I gave her some medicine, and there was nothing else I could do for her. She was very white in the face, and her lips were very grey, and she could not breathe at all, she could not breathe. And I was choked with fury and impotence, and choked with the tears of fury and helplessness and indignation. I remember now when my mother recovered from this attack, I remember now how she began to laugh and she said: Pompey—no, it was Patty, then—Patty, you are choking. And so in the end I began to laugh too. It was all over then for that moment, all was again a calm peacefulness after a great storm of fury and terror. 'All thoughts to rive the heart are here, and all are vain; Horror and scorn and hate and fear and indignation—Oh why did I awake? when shall I sleep again?' This is quite a good verse to say if you are in the Housman mood, but for me it certainly does not express a significant truth. Always the buoyant, ethereal and noble thought is in my mind: Death is my servant.

So I think every sensitive young child should early learn this. It is a great source of strength and comfort. It is so possible that things may become more than we can bear, is it not? That is not my thought at all. But rather, it is so possible we may be afraid that things will become more than we can bear. There is a very deadly poison in the fear that things may become more than we can bear. There is a very deadly sort of slave feeling in this thought. For if we think this and become undone by our fear, we may too anxiously placate our fellow-beings, who appear to us to be in more authoritative positions and to have more power than we over the things that oppress us. But with death as our immediate ally, such thoughts vanish.

Why should the human heart afraid, Utterly undone dismayed, Moaning, from the truth afar, *toion d'apebe tode pragma,* And sitting dumb beneath necessity of hidden fate, Turn up its mournful eyes and weep and wait. For the accustomed end and the deep grave. Slain by itself when but itself could save?

In this poem the suicide slew himself because he was afraid. That is quite the wrong motive. And it is the motive I should be most careful to avoid implanting in the child I am thinking of. It is just as possible to be ignoble in self-slaying as in every other department of human activity. No no it will not do.

To brace and fortify the child who already is turning with fear and repugnance from the life he is born into, it is necessary to say: Things may easily become more than I choose to bear. That is a very healthy and a very positive attitude. But you should point out that the child is at once no longer a Christian. For the thought: Things may easily become more than I *can* bear, leaves him a Christian, if a half hearted, faithless sort of a Christian. The door, as it were ('as it were' as the curate of my childhood used to say) is still half open . . . 'I done it, Lord, but I done it in a moment of temporary insanity, not of *felo de se,* so help me.'

But that 'choose' is a grand old burn-your-boats phrase that will put beef into the little one, and you see if it doesn't bring him to a ripe old age. If he doesn't in the end go off natural I shall be surprised. Well look here, I am not paid anything for this statement, but look here, here am I. See what it's done for me. I'm twice the girl I was that lay crying and waiting for death to come at that convalescent home. No, when I sat up and said: Death has got to come if I call him, I never called him and never have.

So teach your little ones to look on Death as Thanatos-Hades the great Lord of the Dead, that must, great prince though he be, come to their calling. And on the shadowy wings of this dark prince let them be borne upwards from the mire of makeshift and fearful compromise.

'A man must live.' No, there is no compulsion. A man must die. Yes, there are many circumstances in which a man must die. I wrote another poem: There are a great many things I'd rather not be than dead, And this is the thought that runs for ever in my head. When I'm walking alone or lying upon my bed. What's life, friend, that you so much should prize it, Or death that you'd think on it to disguise it, Remembering, not go forth to surprise it? It is the end of life, the end of strife, A rope, a poisoned cup, a knife.

But to witness suffering and not be able to help? How will our little one react to that? All thoughts to wring, excuse me I should say rive, the heart are there.

Well there you must suffer to the utmost of your capacity for suffering with the person who is suffering. Go with them and beware of self pity. All sympathy has in it an element of self pity. I am afraid that cannot be helped. You must just let that go. It cannot be helped. You so much wish to alleviate. That is practical positive and desirable. You cannot. You imagine yourself in the sufferer's place. Already this begins to be dangerous. The livelier your imagination the greater your pity. And the greater your fear. This is already dangerous.

When I saw the suffering of my much loved ma, I could not help her. I raged against necessity I raged against my absconding and very absent pa, I raged and fumed and spat. My emotion I like to think was simple, pure, and vigorous. But was there in it for all that an element of self pity? I came in time to view my absconded pa without indignation. And if at first 'Revenge, Timotheus cried' I later shut up my old Timotheus. My mama had made an unsuitable marriage and no doubt my pa found it also very unsuitable. And unsuitable marriages breed the Pompeys of this world, and a lot of other troubles as well.

* * *

As a baby I was rather cynical. I wrote a poem about it which I will now give you.It will break up the page for you, and something fresh to the eye helps the tired brain and aids concentration. I dare say you find it difficult to concentrate? Never mind, the great thing is never to mind. Just keep on trying, and one day you may figure as a case-sheet in one of those books the smarties write, that have such high-up titles, they would look well on any drawing-room table, like the one I have in mind at this moment—'The Economics of Fatigue and Unrest.' I said The Economics of Fatigue and Unrest. Is not that a sweet title to put in gold ink on a red cloth-board?

Do you, Reader, ever have this suffering feeling of economics and unrest? Do you?

Like hell you do. Well, here is the poem; work it out for yourself:

It was a cynical babe
Lay in its mother's arms,
Born two months too soon,
After many alarms.
Why is its mother sad,
Weeping without a friend?
Where is its father, say?
He tarries in Ostend.
It was a cynical babe. Reader before you condemn, pause:
It was a cynical babe—not without cause.

I have vivid memories of my papa and the war. My papa was then at last in the Navy, and having a very cold and hateful time up off Iceland, or may be it was Greenland. He was so much the very silent service, we really had the vaguest ideas of his whereabouts. But there was something of habit in this, remembering the 'Off to Valparaiso' postcards of which I have already spoken.

But at least during the war we knew papa had gone to a place where it was always—no, not afternoon, but ice and snow. We once had a photograph (this I like to think, for the honour of H.M. Navy, was after the war) of his ship, absolutely draped in several mantles of undriven snow on snow, and the great guns looking like they'd never had shells twisting to destruction along their inside tubes.

My papa hated the cold more than anything. It was certainly too bad. Once he got sent south convoying. That was better. We sent his whites chasing after him and they reached him, poor papa, as he sailed again into hated Scapa. It was certainly all very difficult. And even the convoying was no picnic. The South Africans, hearty over-paid racketeers, simply would not, would not, *my dear*, obey the signals of the irascible British. They thought, like all the poor simple untorpedoed, that all this ballyhoo about lights-out was sheer English uppishness and interference.

However, we got them safely across, as

you know we did, we never lost a convoy. And when they got to standing up on terra firma, wherever it was they got to standing up, no doubt the risks they ran were no greater than the risks they ran a few miles off their home port.

My papa was, among many other duties, in charge of the coding department. And very highly complicated it was, and I often think of him with very real sympathy when I am doing our own, by no means simple, coding at the office. For as with me so with him, the people at the other end are simply not to be relied upon to decode the simplest words. They are sub-mental, *my dear*, absolutely certifiable if their family doctors hadn't been bribed.

However the consequences can be rather serious in an institution like the Royal Navy, when everything depends on the rapid assimilation of coded instructions. So that one day, I hate to relate, the Admiral's ship, *my dear*, the Admiral's ship, if you please, completely failed to respond to a challenge from H.M.S. *Towser*. With what result? With what result, you may well ask. H.M.S. *Towser* fired on the flag ship—and missed.

This was regarded by the Higher Command as a double fault, and no more was said about it. I mean what was there to say, apart from those vivid Anglo-Saxon monosyllables, and a few hundred pounds to the tax payers, what was there to say? We do not courtmartial our admirals nowadays thank God—we've stepped up a bit since the days of Byng Boy and those cads. If we want to *encourager les autres* there are other less barbarous means. And now we will draw to a close, with Free Chairs for Delinquent Bottoms in the shadow of the Admiralty Arch.

Other war memories come crowding back to me now that we are in the shadow of this Anglo-Italian embroglio. William was a friend of the family's.

He joined up in 1914 and in 1915 he was wounded. He was shot in the leg, he was shot. Oh William, how I remember how William got sent to our local hospital, which had been Lord Rumbelow's house until this Lord Rumbelow that did not marry Miss Funnyabove died, and his son died, and there was no one left to wish to keep up the house, that had a lovely high floating portico, that was a lovely palladian house, looking out floatingly over a parkland estate, looking down and over a broad piece of lake water, very still, very deep, with an island in the middle, with an island with trees bending down and lolling upon the lake water. Very beautiful was this parkland, and as a child I had the greatest desire to possess it and to possess the high and lovely house.

Lord Rumbelow used to ride a fine stepping black mare. He used to canter across the broad grass space before the house and above the lake. The mare was a spanking creature, with an easy swift trot, and a canter that made you feel you must have that mare. I never saw her in a gallop. Lord Rumbelow was killed before the war, in a hunting accident. And his son died three weeks later, dying of blood poisoning. His ferret bit him. He was twelve years old, and the only child. So the family sold the house and the estate and moved away into the real country. I think this is where they moved away to, because already Bottle Green was no longer quite the real country.

It still had farm houses standing. It still had woods and covert-shooting, and keepers' cottages. But already the shadow of advancing London was upon it, and though the war stayed the advance, the armistice already saw the builders at busy work, and the streets of houses going up, and the paving stones going down. And presently it was already a suburb.

But I am very grateful, and it is with great gratitude that I remember, that the suburban council bought the house and land from Lord Rumbelow, and turned the house as it was into a service hospital for convalescent wounded, and bought the park, and made a public park of it, making no alterations whatever. And this was very splendid and refraining of them, making no alterations except this: they put a railing around the lake. And this I think had to be done, because the lake was in a hollow, was very large and deep and dangerous, and children playing might easily run down and fall into the lake, which was curious too in this way, it was not shallow at all at the edge, but already very deep. In places it was twenty foot deep, and there were also undersurface currents, also very dangerous and treacherous, so that never could people swim in this lake, it was too dangerous.

Lord Rumbelow's house and estate had a beautiful name too, it was called Scapelands and is still called Scapelands, but now it is called Scapelands Park. But it is not at all ever looking as parks most generally look.

Most parks—there is the one I know at Ipswich, there is the one I faintly remember in Hull. They have, first they have not a lake, but it is only a pond, it has cement sides and a cement bottom, it has also very ugly iron spikes for railings. Whereas Scapelands lake, although so deep and so treacherous and so dangerous, has only a not-so ugly bar railing, with white wooden posts at intervals.

But then this *usual* park, it has also, it is sure to have, a shrubbery, and it has flower beds of course, very neat and the flowers are geraniums. And then it has, it is sure to have, a little hillock somewhere, and on the top of this hillock there is a rustic gardenhouse, where sometimes, if it is very large, there is a lock-up cupboard, where twig brooms are kept for sweeping the falling leaves from the asphalt paths that this *usual* park has. And also there people can sit too, if it is the large rustic house, when it rains.

Then also this *usual* park has a section set apart for sports. There is the tennis section, and the children's play-ground section. And the people who say that children's voices are the purest music certainly ought to be the people who sit near children's playgrounds. And they ought to sit there and put down something else about the way children's voices are sounding. I think they should face right up to how children's voices are sounding, because, though thinking this way about children's voices is not perhaps in itself of great moment, it can later lead to very serious obliquity of the mental vision. So go sit in the children's playground and think that you will never again blink the facts.

So William was lying in bed, in this beautiful Scapelands house. And now I remember it was snow on the ground. It was December. It was a very hard winter, that one was, and very hard was the ground, and the cart ruts, going along to the hospital by the other entrance, were quite hard, and so strong you might walk along the top of them. They would not crumble at all. So William's sister Elizabeth wrote to us. And my mother, and Auntie the lion of course, pranced up, my mother in her bath chair, the lion *poussant*, to see William in his hospital bed. And William was being a very great nuisance, and a stumbling block to the V.A.D. nurses. Very prejudicial to discipline was William, because he had a sort of arrangement dementia, and everything must be put, it *must be put* just so.

First his books must be put in his locker, just so. And his apple to eat. And His Fullers peppermint fondants. And his antiseptic sponger. And the extra cover to his hot water bottle. They must be arranged just so. And always the nurse, who was a Bottle Green family, she was called Miss Champagne, she was getting so exasperated. It was too bad. And William sat up in his bed, propped up with pillows, and he was looking rather like George III, very fair, with a round face. The face was rather fat, his eyes were blue, and the nose was rather sharp for a rather fat, but not at the same time *very* fat face. His nose was perhaps rather sharp.

William's expression when Miss Champagne was getting so exasperated was very peculiar, very much his own way of looking. There was something in this expression that was saying: Why is the woman getting exasperated? Is it exasperated? It cannot be *exasperated,* she has absolutely no reason to be looking exasperated. I have shown her so many times, how the apple must go there. But *I* am not looking exasperated, though always I am telling her: The apple must go there. So it is not she who has anything to be exasperated about.

And then there would also be a look on his face that was saying: It is a pity that she cannot understand. It is not anything perhaps to become ferocious about. But it is a pity she cannot understand how it is that the apple must go there. It is just perhaps one of those things in this life that there is no help for.

And there would come into his eyes a look of sadness and fortitude, and perhaps a little of patience. And his eyes would disengage themselves and withdraw. But this withdrawal was perhaps a withdrawal into the outside of himself and of time, a withdrawal into the *Ewigkeit*.

And the person of William, and the lineaments of his face in their pain and weakness, might be allowed to say: It is the tears of things and our mortality touches us. But his mind you knew was soaring far above and away from the penalties of the bodily life, in a grand act of dissociation from this bodily life. Where the apple was never put where it should be, on the second shelf where it would not be infected by the peppermint of the fondants.

But on the second shelf. Very slowly and very patiently, and over and over again, he had explained it to Miss Champagne: *On the second shelf*, in front of a book that was at this time a very great favourite of William's, a book that was a book by Khomjakoff on the mystical philosophy of the Russian Orthodox church.

I must just tell you now how this was a very inseparable companion at this time of William's, and later he must lend it to my mother, and so it was this way I came to read it too. I was now twelve, and I copied out a page from this book and this I have found: it is this:

The church and her members know by the inner knowledge of faith the unity and incomprehensibility of her spirit which is indeed the spirit of God. The power of reason alone cannot grasp God's truth, the weakness of man becomes evident in the inadequacy of argument, the church is manifested neither as scripture nor as tradition nor as works, but she bears witness of herself in scripture. For Christ knows what is his, and the church also wherein he dwells knows by innate conviction, and cannot help but know the outward expression of her own life. Oh Lord relent, deliver, forgive, cleanse my heart, Oh Lord renew a right spirit within me. Enter my Life and revive my deadness. Enter my physician and heal my wounds—here there is a word I cannot read; it goes on—and kindle in my heart a fiery love of thee. Enter my King to be enthroned in my heart and rule thou there. Thou alone art my King and my Lord. This is a prayer by Demetrius of Rostoff that William had written out and put in this other book that he later lent to my mother and so I came to read it.

This is the way I came to read this book and how I came to read this prayer of Demetrius, and how at this time I was striving myself so hard to get into the inside-of this Christian religion, that, if you *can*, you can into the inside-of like you cannot get into the inside-of the pagan religion. Because that has passed away, and any conscious seeking after it must be a revival, no, not a revival, because there is life in that word, but a feeling that is false in this seeking after the passed away pagan religion, that is false, that cannot come to good.

And was the good pagan ever so much inside-of his religion as the good Christian is inside-of his? I cannot think so. The simple prayer of the Christian which is the essence of the Christian religion: O God make me a better man, could not have been prayed by a pagan. That is peculiarly a Christian attitude. But at this time I was trying very hard. Yes at this time I was pushing and forcing myself to get into the inside-of this Christian religion. But all the time at this time I was feeling cold, very cold and outside-of, and not at all ever warm and inside-of.

And oh how I admired the bishops of the Church of England because all the time they seem to be inside-of and not outside-of, and at the same time they are intellectual and scholarly, and not sentimentalizing, and not thinking of the everlasting arms that are underneath, like it was everlasting feather bed.

So I was thinking how it was they got this way, and stayed there; and all the time, at the back of my mind was the idea of death, like it was the idea personified, like it was the idea of Thanatos the god, that was yet to come at a call, but not a god you could pray to certainly to make you a better man.

But not either with the necessary idea that death is annihilation, but toying with that possibility too, though remembering that 'the doctrine of the eternity of the universe is compatible with the view that every individual in it perishes, the type alone persisting and renewing itself in successive individuals. P. however asserts positively that there are ideas of individuals, and since the phenomenal world derives whatever reality it has from the Ideas, this is conclusive and therefore indestructible. Nothing that really is can every perish. OUDEN APOLAITAI ONTON.'

Well and who is this 'P'. that goes round making these positive assertions? Well this P. is, well have a guess, have a guess, he was a bit A.D. but not so much. And the man I am quoting is that noble Dr. I. that was writing yesterday, to-day, and forever in the. Well see here Mr. Wedding-Guest-Reader, you got to do some work.

And all the time I was admiring the bishops of the Church of England, and especially that saintly bishop that was Bishop of Oxford, that, being asked to preach to the troops before going into action, that had the sense not to talk about glory and death, and greater love, and *esprit de corps*, and all that line, that has been trod out to weariness and the scent of bitter death. And not like death, not like I mean *Thanatos*, but just death with a yawn on his face, looking downright common, like the man that's called and won't be put off any longer, like the man that's called, and this time he will have the slap-up new-idea electric washing-up machine, he will have it, and take it away, and prayers and tears won't save your loved electric machine that is such a good Idea, because there are already so many instalments owing and you cannot pay. And he is very common, he is very common, very disagreeable and very determined. So away he goes with that washing-up machine that was a good idea.

That is the way death is made to look when heavy-handed pompous and cruel men get on to the subject. But this great bishop he was not like that at all, he just stood up and spoke to the men about to go into action, he just spoke to them about tithes and first fruits. That took them out of themselves and got them thinking there were other problems just as pressing as theirs.

Oh the really great Christians are very admirable, very quiet. So later on I was reading *John Inglesant* and if ever I came near to getting into the inside-of the Christian religion it was then. 'The cross of Christ is composed of many crosses, is the centre, the type, the essence of all crosses. We must suffer with Christ whether we believe in him or not. We must suffer for the sins of others as for our own; and in this suffering we find a healing and purifying power and element.

That is what gives to Christianity in its simplest and most unlettered form, its force and life. Sin and suffering for sin; a sacrifice itself mysterious offered mysteriously to the divine nemesis or Law of Sin, dread, undefined, unknown, yet sure and irresistible with the iron necessity of law. This the intellectual Christ, the Platonic-Socrates, did not offer; hence his failure and the success of the Nazarene. *Vicisti, Galilaee.'*

So this is funny now I read this over, with the other quotation, both copied at such separated intervals. Now I think this is clear for the first time. It is no further than the neoplatonic idea of Christ that I can come. That is the nearest. That is how I am hankering after the inside-of position but getting just this near to it and no nearer.

I think a great many people nowadays cannot get into the inside-of position but then they say: It is the fault of the Church. And by and by the Church gets thinking: It is our fault. It certainly is punk of the Church of England to think that way. So then they say: we will cut out doctrine, and step down among the people, and not preach at all, but just have a good heart-to-heart talk, just ordinary men among men, just a helpful chat Sunday evenings, just not clever at all, but simple as abc, and just being kind and just being kind and.

Oh I hate that. That is very base and treacherous. That is making a desert and a howling waste of the church. That is making the Church of England all Arizona and salt deserts. That is, that certainly is, a fault, whatever the good kind motive of it is, that is a very serious fault, that is making the church of England the very heart of the fiend, all dust and ashes, and the heart of the fiend, with yawning and cracking of fingerjoints. Oh it is all so boring there in the heart of the fiend, in the salt desert of Arizona. That is a mistake.

Then there is that part of the Church of England where William belonged, where it is being very full of incense and ritual, very attractive, very warm and alive, very alive-o it is there, and they are telling you about the meaning and significance of ritual. And that is a little bit difficult at first, but attractive too, because it seems that by and by you are going to understand something that is much more than the significance of ritual, you are going to understand something that is much more than that, so you listen, you prick up your ears, you listen, you are full of hope.

But by and by you see it is nothing so much more than that. Oh is it our fault? Yes, partly it is our fault, because so often we are saying, we are crying down the intellect. So this way it is our fault too. We are saying we are not clever at all, and taking pride that we are not clever. But we are clever enough when it comes to being clever in ways that it pays to be clever, we are not so stupid there.

But now I think the Church should stand up, should get right up now, and say: Stupidity is a sin. And then it should teach in very difficult to understand, very high-up language, not simple at all, but really very difficult, and it should teach the philosophy of Christianity in very high-up terms, and it should always speak high-up and well above people's heads, so they have trouble to understand. And then the church might be empty. Very good, let it be empty. But by and by people would get sick at the way they missed the point, and they would get on their mettle, and be clever. Well think, the clever way they do the crossword puzzles, like the clever way they grapple with Torquemada, and the intricacies of the Stock Exchange, and the intricacies of, well say the intricacies of the law of libel, which certainly is not easy to get the hang of, and the intricacies of, well say the intricacies of Somerset House, and the problems of taxation and economics. Well think now how many people in their separate way grapple with these difficult problems, which are departments of the mind, which are the same departments of the mind that would be called in to grapple with the problems of Christian apologetics. And was St. Paul simply having Sunday evening chats not-a-bit-clever? Not he. He certainly was a clever one, was St. Paul, very profound and cunning.

Well let the Church think it is a non-Christian land, where the people are bone lazy about using their brains, but good enough at it if they're interested, and not only materially interested either, but knowing in a dim dark way sometimes that, but knowing that, only in using their minds to the utmost, and more, will they escape the fiend's heart of boredom. And let the Church go round and about, being very high-up in their preaching very deep and don't care, very; Don't-care-if-it-is-above-you, stretch-a-bit-you-lazy-hound. And not a bit affable and simple, and not very kind, but very deep and ingenious. Well look then they might try this. It certainly would be a change.

Well there was William sitting up in his bed, looking like George III, looking like George Three with a pin stuck in him, looking like George looking like he was cross. And William had a natural gift for religion. He was high church, which I so much prefer to Anglican, because it takes you straight back to Laud, and that little word anglican, or as they say anglo-catholic, takes you slap up into a little clique, that is being good fun if you have a mind that likes playing cliques and secret societies.

And it is funny how they do, and how everybody that is speaking or writing about this movement gets called by his initials, very intimate and friendly, or by some nickname, also very intimate and friendly. Like I mean Ronny Knox for Fr. R. Knox, late of this persuasion, now lost to us, ahem, in the Italian mission, and in the devious ways of crossword puzzles, and no, not crossword puzzles so much as *acrostics*, and the kind of detective story that is but, chaps, an extension of the acrostic habit. And they had a great feeling, very high and warm it was, for Father, I now forget his name, that had suffered some time ago, when people got the option of suffering that way of their opinions. He was also very high and Anglican, this Father and got sent to prison when Queen Victoria was thinking: All this ritual is such nonsense. Like my Aunt says: Such nonsense—don't talk to *me*.

Well now this suffering for your opinions, I never could quite get the hang of this. But this too I think is my fault, the way I cannot get into the inside-of Christian religion is being my fault. I certainly have a flippant and frivolous mind, I certainly get worse having this flippant and frivolous mind the older I get.

I certainly am fundamentally not serious, the way the French use it, not serious, though I have had my chance, when I think of William and his friends. There was Tommy for instance used to come round to our house, and other friends of William's. They used to come round and sit on our sofas and settees and chairs and hassocks, and after that on the floor, and they used to talk. And I, how old was I then? It was later on in the war, I must have been 14 or 15, and I used to sit and listen and talk too, and then at this time I certainly had my chance of getting serious, but always there was something in me that was fundamentally not serious; like my English mistress at school wrote of me when I showed up an essay on Mark Antony.

I said, to begin with I said just this. Chaps, then I could write, it was certainly stuff you could read in the papers, read in the papers. So it began: 'Brilliant irresponsible Mark Antony.' And there was a lot more like that. I got written at the end of this essay: 'You have no appreciation of the better qualities of man.' Well, that made me think, couldn't I get to be serious? But no, I could not. But hadn't I the chance in a thousand, sitting listening to William and Tommy, and there was Captain Poltallock that did my Latin homework for me?

You see these people were practising Christians, really good. And there was something very sweet about them too. But always, well I couldn't be altogether completely serious, but I tried hard, I assure you I took this remark about the better qualities of man, lack of appreciation of, very seriously, and I was always trying to get things from a serious angle and sometimes I used to get downright morbid, chaps, I used to sit and cry, thinking there I was like Goethe's Mephistopheles, the spirit that denies.

How it was you may well ask. I used to sit and think of Rome under the emperors, and not the good emperors either. Because, have you ever thought, there were good emperors too. But all good things come to an end, and the same goes for all bad things. So let's not look on the dark side. But that's where I used to be, sitting thinking about Rome under—well, take a medium good-bad emperor, say, well hell, say Tiberius that was good, well he was good at, well wasn't he? Well, take Tiberius, and suppose you were a Christian going suffering for his opinions. But always when I was supposing I was a Christian, I would get running round Rome like I was not a Christian at all, but just one of those Romans that have lost their investments and are living on their wits and on their friends.

But see now, this suffering for your opinions—if you go to your own place anyway? I guess this about going to your own place was a very pregnant remark, it certainly is full of significance. So they say, whoever it was said: You go to your own place. Well that's the idea, see? You are bad, pretend you are bad, but you go round talking like you was good. No good at all. It's what's written on the heart that counts.

Ah so. Well then it cuts the other way too? Suppose now, just pretend you're good, and go round talking like you was bad. No good at all. It's what's written on the heart that counts. So then why go subjecting your beautiful body, that is a good friend to you, and is putting up always with a lot of, a hell of a lot of rough handling, like drinking with meals and keeping sitting up late hours like Harriet and me—why subject it to the tortures of the damned just to show your opinions, when it's what's written on the heart that counts, and the thing that really counts is what is making you all the time, and forming you into being the sort of definite person that, clear as if it was labelled, has its own place to go to? And what is so important is what you are selecting all the time and discarding as the years go on, making yourself into this sort of a very definite person, with his own place to go to. And if he goes to that place, how can he be anything but happy? For in this world of catch-as-catch-can we are so often being in the place that is certainly *not* our place at all, and so being unhappy.

Oh I can understand well enough suffering for your opinions in this way, I will show you that I often have suffered for my opinions. There are some things I feel so strongly about, I can hardly find the words to tell the people that don't think this way, how I feel that for them they might as well die, in fact it would be better that they had never been born. I mean for instance a certain type of vulgarity.

When I am confronted with this certain type of vulgarity, embodied in a certain type of vulgarian, I can feel I am a tiger, with claws on his feet that would go ripping and tearing the flesh from off him. There is a real white-hot flame of heat and light in this hatred which I feel when I am confronted with a certain type of vulgarity, allied with stupidity, which results in a very base sort of cruelty. No, I do not consider the tiger-clawing feeling to be cruelty. That is just a flash and a flame that would scorch up and calcine this clod, like the Russians say liquidate.

> 'If nothing skills I cannot help my case
> 'Tis the Last Judgment's fire must cure this place,
> Calcine its clods and set my prisoners free.'

That is how I feel, nothing less, when I meet this sort of person. I feel I am an instrument of God, that is not altogether the Christian god; that I am an instrument of this God that must *calcine these clods,* that are at the same time stupid and vulgar, and set free this God's prisoners, that are swift, white and beautiful and very bright and flaming-fierce.

So what do I mean by this vulgarity and stupidity? There was once a man that read Swinburne. This boy had read Swinburne. So? So that's the boy that read Swinburne. And by and by he was still never getting any further than being the boy that read Swinburne. But by and by I remember he was also reading Kipling. That gave him a line on the army. And he remembered he read the Bible. That gave him a line on Kipling again, and a touch of style that was spread very cleverly indeed. He certainly was a clever boy. Upon nothing, very thin and fine, was the spreading. Over and upon nothing.

He then set up as a man of taste, refinement and education. He'd even heard of A. Huxley, D. H. Lawrence and Les Sitwells. He said: They ought to be crucified. Very pat he was with these fine old masculine phrases, very pat indeed, and very mum and dumb about contemporary writers and artists. It was splendid, simply spendid, chaps, the way this boy would see the horses home before he laid a bet. But D.H.L. and A.H. and Les Sitwells, well, they were safe for a heave-ho half-a-brick anywhere he went. And of course, *my dear,* he was 'a bit of a writer myself'. 'Oh yes you know I *write,* you know, just straightforward and honest. It's a job like any other job, isn't it? Only harder, harder than a navvy's job. It's just a job JOB JOB.' You'd think he sat there all day and night writing the Encyclopaedia Britannica.

And what was all this hard hard work? *My dear,* the boy was a Lady Novelist. The only surviving Lady Novelist. That's what this boy was that read Swinburne, that got his line on the army, like it was Ouida writing. You'd think British Officers sat all day just keeping their backs straight and their faces in profile, just having slightly greying hair and cynical blue eyes. Cynical blue eyes and thinning grey hair—that was this boy that read Swinburne, that was this boy's projection of himself.

But what was the job job job that this only surviving lady novelist was doing with his projection of himself, the middle-aged, distinguished, I'll say distinguished soldierly figure, with cynical blue eyes and thinning grey hair? What was his bread-and-butter job job job? Well, chaps, there he was. Oh come on, Pompey, what was he writing? Well, chaps you see, there he was writing those chic little middles for girlies' papers, the tuppenny weekly girlies' papers that are always having emotional crises, and wondering about their young man. And wondering.

This boy that read Swinburne, this lady novelist-cum-soldier out of Clarksons, was what I was meaning when I said, you can suffer for your opinions all you have to, by having to have people like these people, that are so god-awful stupid and yet you cannot slip them a k.o., but have to suffer in silence, not being always able even.—Oh they are all about and around, and when they are, as this boy is, stuffed up with *männlicher Protest* and pseudomasculine buck, that is very difficult, that makes me cold and furious, that is all the suffering I have to do, to get all the suffering that's all the suffering that is my quota, just not being able to forget they are there.

And now there is in my memory, clear and beautiful as a preservèd plant, under a glass dome, there is William sitting up in his convalescent hospital bed, looking like Hanoverian George, looking like George III had a pin stuck in him. But there was something sweet about William and we were then to go on being friends. Because this was quite *platonisch,* and quite steering clear and uncomplicated by sex.

Now William is always running through my life, something that is very quiet and strong. He is living now in Bury St. Wash, that is a little town by the sea in Lincs, and it is where I am going down and staying with him week-ends, for years, at often quite long intervals. But it does not matter.

And now I will describe this week-end with him that has just passed. It was a very good week-end and a great relief and a respite from the strain I have been having for some months past being engaged to darling Freddy who is also very sweet. But being engaged and under the approaching shadow of marriage does not make him so-o-o sweet, indeed it does not. So often with the sweet boys I have had, I have taken them to Bury St. Wash to see William. And sometimes yes it is all splendid, splendid, chaps. And sometimes it is not. But Freddy has to come. He has to come next week-end but one, and we shall enjoy ourselves. We had better.

I was feeling sad as I was travelling to Bury St. Wash, because I was thinking: I cannot marry Freddy, and I was thinking: I have already broken off this funny-ha-ha engagement business, that is always being such an aggravation and a dirge for us both, and now again I cannot break it off, because I shall be looking as if I was always changing my mind.

But then I was at Bury and William met me with the car, and took me back and he said 'Pompey, we will go and have some nice hot coffee, it is very good, and some biscuits, and then we will go out and have a ride round in the car, and in the evening you must come and see two German friends of mine.'

So there was a nice fire in his room and already I was feeling better. William now has a house to himself in the suburban part of

Bury, and he is doing his own cooking and housekeeping. You know I was feeling a waif, sitting there, but afterward we were drinking coffee, and I will say now that William makes excellent coffee, and rightly prides himself on his coffee, so afterwards we were drinking a very great deal of this excellent coffee, and eating a very great many ginger biscuits, that were rather flabby I remember, but the ginger flavour was still left. And if they had lost that hard brittleness that young ginger biscuits have, I did not say so, I was feeling very kind and mellowed myself by now, and I should not have been so unkind as to say: William, your biscuits are flabby. No.

Then we went round and about and to another little town that was called Skye Blue, and bought a large steak-and-kidney pie to be warmed up in the oven. Only as things turned out we did not eat that pie at all, so now no doubt William is now eating steak-and-kidney pie. It will last him alone through the week until Thursday. So William said: Tell me everything. So everything I told him, for I had not seen him for eighteen months. So I will tell you all that I told William.

I said: You remember Josephine? Well, it is funny about Josephine. She is somehow sweet, there is something sweet about Josephine. And she is lovely to stay with, she has a lovely cookie and she gives me lovely pale apricot sheets, and the bedroom is looking very nice. She is lovely to stay with, as Harriet is lovely to stay with, but of course they are not resembling each other in any other way.

Harriet is like me, and. And Josephine is not like me, but.

Josephine is my friend, and was my very intimate friend, but now her husband died and so she has moved a little away to be in the country. When Josephine is telling that story I cry. She is such a very good little *raconteuse,* I will tell you later. So Josephine since her husband died has left London, where she was always entertaining rather titled people, and living a rather titled existence, and not verging on the boheem at all, but being very orthodox, and being very orthodoxly very best City out of South Kensington and very sound, *chic* and *rangée.* Josephine is now living in the country by the sea with her little girl who is called Reine. So I am telling William about Josephine, and how there is this, and this, and how there was this. While I was staying with Josephine at Easter she gave a children's party, for rather older children. It was on Good Friday, and we were all the time playing those games; you have two knitting needles and you take broad beans out of a jar, or you have chopsticks. But that is easy if you have eaten with chopsticks.

Eaten with chopsticks. There is a café in Berlin I am thinking of at this moment. It is a Japanese café, but it is not at all reminding you of the church bazaar, when all the ladies, who are not any longer very young they say: We must have a fancy dress, though often their own dresses are so looking that way, it does not seem necessary, but they say: We must have a fancy dress. And so sure enough oh Jesus Christ it has to be Japanese or Dutch.

Oh this café in Berlin is not looking that way at all. It is very severely restrained, with a very great and strengthening and bracing austerity, and there in that café I was one evening with Karl, eating with chopsticks. And I was wearing a black hat and coat, very sombre, and a printed grey and black and white chiffon scarf tied like a handkerchief round the collar. And presently a man outside looking in, saw Karl and myself sitting there, looking at each other. And the man was selling roses. So he smiled and came in, and he was carrying a great armful of dark red roses, and he spoke to Karl, and Karl bought the roses for me, and Karl looked at me smiling and said: *Das geht. Das geht.*

How red those roses were against the black and the white, and the silvered oak tables, with no other colour at all, I can remember now very vividly, and the smiling face of Karl, and the waiters very silently bowing, bowing, bowing, over folded hands.

So I have eaten with chopsticks. But at this older children's party that Josephine gave, later we played charades. And a child who was already very nearly grown up, she was about sixteen or seventeen, said it would be amusing to act the word *tartlet*, and for *tart*, it would be possible to put on a red *beret*, and to prance along, and to look forwards and backwards, and to give the old-fashioned look, and to be a tart. But Josephine said: No. And I thought certainly it would not do, at a children's party, where the children were not alone, acting their own choice of words to themselves, but officially at least as it were countenanced and supported by aunts and parents, all present there together. But that was not why Josephine said: No. She left me in no doubt why she said: No. It was one of the funniest things that Josephine had ever said. It was so funny, I will just tell you and leave it. She said: No we cannot do a word like that. Because it is Good Friday.

So when I told William this, he laughed so much. He said: Pompey, I cannot believe that. It is too funny. You are making it up. And I said: No, but thank you very much, but I could not make up anything so funny as that.

And then I went off into a blue doze, sitting there in the car next to William. I was thinking about Josephine who is also this very dear friend of mine. And I certainly do have a lot of good friends, and I certainly am a very lucky but spoilt and ungrateful girl. I am a desperate character. But how this has recently been brought again home to me, I will presently say.

Meanwhile here I am thinking of Josephine. She is small, about my size but not so thin, and she has mixed English colouring, brownish-fair hair, very soft and sleek, and blue eyes, that are getting a little cold sometimes. This English *Blondheit* is so unlike the soft gentle loving and giving *Blondheit* of the soft gentle loving and giving German women. It has a lot of self-pride in it, and can be very bitterly ruthless and very furious too sometimes, and unkind, carrying on the unkindness from year to year. Very stiff, stubborn and unyielding. A man might break his head against that, and his heart too.

But this week-end at Easter when I was staying with Josephine she was telling me again and again about her family, and how rakish the cousin is, and how *stürmisch* and oppressive her Aunt, who is always so very extravagant, and having to come and stay and stay with Josephine, because she has run through her allowance, and there is still a lot of the year to be got through. It is so unfortunate that never will the year keep up with the allowance. The year certainly suffers from time lag. Why look at that allowance, it can do a year in two months and then there is still ten months. And so is it not tough for Josephine to have to make up the year's discrepancies? And I say yes, it is punk for Josephine and I sit beside her, and she drives and drives furiously and relentlessly, through all the country roads and lanes, and all the time she is saying things like this: Pompey, my Aunt is a very extravagant woman. You will indeed be fortunate if you never have to learn what it means to be the only niece of an extravagant woman.

And gradually, stroke by stroke, the portrait of the extravagant woman is painted. It is very vivid; oh Keith oh Keith of Ravelston, The sorrows of thy line. Always there is a great deal of this undertoning Josephine's conversation. Oh proud heart and insufficient purse. Oh mother of unworthy Gracci. Oh children of sour-grape-eating parents. Oh lamentable cousin and too favoured younger brother. Oh sickness, and war, and love, and death. All this Josephine is telling me, and the sun is shining down on the fox-red bracken, and the paths go off into the woods, but we follow follow follow the white road, and the misfortunes of parents, the wickedness of uncles, the extravagance of aunts and the indifference of cousins.

And all the time in the back of the car there is the little child Reine, the most beautiful little child I have ever seen, with a fresh precise mind, and an eye for detail and a practical fastidiousness that she has from her mother.

She takes me round the garden: This is spinach and these are loganberries, and these are Uncle Ivor's begonias, no silly Auntie Pompey, not those, these. And yesterday I went out on my bicycle, and to-day I shall be going to tea with Daphne and Paula, and to-morrow I am going to dig in my garden. But to-day it is too wet.

And in Winchester Cathedral she looks at the tomb of Cardinal Beaufort: What is he doing there? Is he dead? Is it a long time ago? Is he with God? Then why is he here?

In the streets of Winchester holding my hand she suddenly breaks away, and I collide with a Canon: O darling, I say to Reine, do look where you are going. But the Canon was, I can see it in his outraged blue eyes, for one moment he was thinking I was speaking to him.

We have tea in a cake shop with a fine old rustic air, and a fine old rustic way with the bill. It is very pleasant and very *married-lady-without-husband* all the time I am with Josephine. Before her husband died, when they lived in town, I used to meet a great many Fleet Street personalities at her house, and people in the English and American magazine publishing worlds. Because at that time there was no Reine, and Josephine was editing a magazine.

She and Harriet are my only two office friends, but Josephine has left now a long time, and lives in a little town by the sea. It is so like a suburb, a very good residential district you know. It is funny but always Josephine is being very good in residences and in social contacts. She has great strength of purpose, and knows exactly what she wants from life, and knows the way to set about to get it.

Her mind runs in a clear straight channel, she never wastes her energy, she never wastes her time. She is passionate, has great integrity and is relentless in pursuit. She is a formidable woman, but where her feelings go she is a most faithful friend.

And all the time I so much like to taste her life, to sample it and consider it, and all the time it is not my life at all.

Oh to taste, sample, flavour—how much of my life is spent in this enjoyable frivolity. How greatly I enjoy for a week-end, for a week, perhaps for a fortnight, to savour the lives of my friends. They are all so very different from each other my friends, they are not at all alike, and cannot even safely be set down in front of each other. Show me a man's friends and I will show you the man. Then what sort of a *man* is Pompey whose friends are 'all of different kinds'? Is there any Pompey at all? Is Pompey a chimera, a creature such as Lord Mellifont in *The Private Life*, whose existence depended on the presence of his friends?

I am now feeling very sad and dashed about this problem, though for most of my time it certainly never occurs to me to bother me. But now I fall away from thinking very *sympatisch* thoughts about *chère* Josephine, I fall back, and again in the car with William I am facing myself, and I am, oh how am I to—?

'You ride your friendships lightly, Pompey,'

William has said this to me. And: 'You are wonderful', laughing, 'you are wonderful, Pompey, it is amazing how adaptable you are, how you can get on with everybody.'

And this is how I am feeling, sad and *stürmisch*. Yes certainly I can get on with everybody, but I am never wanting to get on with them for very long, and yet I love them. But I must go. I love them and also I love the memory and thought of them. And just as I must go, so after a time, after another time, I must come back to them.

My friendships, they are a very strong part of my life, they are as light as gossamer but also they are as strong as steel. And I cannot throw them off, nor altogether do with them or without them. And I love them at the point when they say: It is nice to see you again. And I love them too at the point when they say: Good-bye, come again soon.

The rhythm of friendship is a very good rhythm. But now I am involved again in love, and I must marry, or I must not marry. And the rhythm of friendship is now so strong in my blood; I must go, I must come back. Here I am again. Now I am going.

And this rhythm is antipathetic to marriage, and it is not very successful in love without marriage, always it has been making a great deal of trouble for me in the past, for all my life. For they do not always feel as I do, that first they must go and then they must come back, and for them it is often not at the same time gossamer-light and steel-strong. It is steel-strong while it is in full current, but afterwards for them it is perhaps not anything at all. While for me it is gossamer-light while it is in full current and steel-strong at the same time. But the steel-strong is not then apparent, and I am happy and laugh a lot, and do not think about the steel-strongness at all.

But after, when perhaps they have gone, at once the gossamer lightness falls away and the steel stays and is apparent. And this causes a great deal of sadness and wildness and despair. And you turn this way and that way, and there is nothing, there is nothing to be done at all, for all the wildness and tears and despair. You have lost. Suddenly you have lost everything, and the hours are long, and only a thousand hours will at all help to heal. *Les heures s'écoulent,* so slowly, minute by minute, and the friends are very kind and say: Time is the only doctor. And it is true. But he is certainly a slow worker that Time, and no anaesthetist at all. And you sit and cry and wring your hands and cry: *Soll ich niemals wieder ruhig sein.* Never, never, nevermore. Quoth the Raven.

Oh the orgy of *stürmisch* sadness of despair and death. And after the thousand hours, and the thousand hours and one, it is again all right, it is again quite all right, and the waggish Pompey prances forth, and the lover now in memory becomes a friend, whose memory is delightful though never my he be seen again.

I have never neglected the altars of Venus, nor avoided her *supplices,* certainly I rate this goddess very highly and have never refused an encounter, nor treated her so impiously as Mr. Bosch, and that sort of person, that use her as a means for promoting the healthful action of the glands. *Oh Venus implacable, oh détestable pensée.*

Already you see my thoughts are turning to that poem-play I always must read when the pains of love displace its pleasures. And what play is this? It is Racine's *Phèdre,* round whose unhappy family I have written the longest poem I have written, taking for its title his line: *La Fille de Minos et de Pasiphaě.* I have seen this play produced once at the Arts Theatre Club, with Sybil Thorndike in the name part, and very excellent she was, most surprisingly to me excellent, for I have never cared for her in the two other plays I most clearly remember, *The Trojan Women,* in translation, and Shaw's *St. Joan.* But in *Phèdre,* in *Phèdre,* there she was very good.

I am not very receptive to The Theatre. There are very few plays I can remember to have a very vivid recollection of them. And for plays in verse, they give me for the most part a very depressing sense of unreality, very depressing, very painful. This is what I find with Shakespeare, where the verse is conventional and the feeling is so warm and so human and so disturbing. For me this in an antithesis which I do not make a response to, except to feel distraught and ill at ease. But in Racine there is no feeling of antithesis, the verse and the emotion are perfectly at one, they fuse perfectly and effect the purgation which is the essence of tragedy.

It is perhaps more in the vein of comedy the number of times in my life I have now already read *Phèdre*, in great distress of mind for a finished love-life. It is now very many times, and now I know this play very well indeed, and for the tragedy and the simplicity of Phèdre I have a very profound feeling. But oh how sure I am that it is so much better to have love with all its pains and terrors and fanaticism than to live untouched the life of the vegetable. But how it tears one, and how *unruhig* it is.

And now I have just been seeing *Romeo and Juliet*. But does that make the same noble elevating and loamishly-sad feeling in me? No, it does not. Again I am distraught and embarrassed by the complications and maladroitness of the plot, but chiefly by its complications.

The plot of a tragedy must be bone-straight and simple. And that is not. And the poetry is thwarted at every turn by the complications of this plot, and even the genius of the nurse's character, and the genius of the lines she speaks, are a distraction. And the so-famous Queen Mab speech of Mercutio's that is a distraction and not a relief. And the play is a very young play of Shakespeare's, and there is a great deal of *minorelizabethanismus* in it, all the horrors and the bones and the charnel house, and Juliet's morbidity when she visualizes in such bludgeoning, strapping, head-smashing words all those things she would rather *not* do, but would rather *not* do than to lose her love. And the tomb scene itself is at once a *minorelizabethanismus,* and also a shadow of the later born Hamlet.

Are not all Shakespeare's plays really versions, schemes and ghosts of Hamlet? But here the echo from the future is so clear, the dead girl, no matter if later she rises, the dead girl and the two men at war upon her bier. It is interesting. I am glad to have seen this. But it is an evening of irritation, I feel, of exasperation, as if one were sided irrevocably with the verse, striving so hard to rise above the clash and clamour of inessentials. How often I have spoken about this with Harriet, but she is open and receptive to the genius of Shakespeare, and I am not, and it it my loss I make no mistake. But it is nothing that can be learnt or had for wishing.

But thou, O spirit of Life, 'thy friends are exultations, agonies And love and man's unconquerable mind'. And I am down to earth again. And my feet are on the earth. And the practical, the convenient, the reasonable, the expedient, must be all my thought, how to tell William, sitting driving beside me in this car through the lanes and roads of Lincs Lincs Lincs—I think of easy rhymes: Leafless Lincs for lovely drinks. Is not this advertisement-land full of easy rhymes?

I think of the easy rhyme I thought of the other day, sitting opposite dark faced smiling Sir Phoebus, at that moment at loss for a phrase succintly to discourage but not offend the too-protestant old school-friend would-be author:

Astarte, Gave a Party, In Cromarty, Everyone was Rather Hearty.

Quite suddenly you see, quite simply, there you are, there. I laugh. Sir Phoebus lifts an inquiring eyebrow. I tell him I have made a poem. I say it to him. He laughs: 'Oh to hell with the old school pal,' he says, 'finish him off for me.'

Finishing off Old Etonians; writing to boring relations; writing speeches, writing writing writing; seeing government officials 'about land tenure in the Argentine', about 'mining rights in Alaska', about shipment of religious statue home to France—a gesture (generous too the thing cost him 100 guineas), on Sir Phoebus's part 'to make his soul'; paying servants, doing accounts, coding and decoding, walking dogs, writing charitable publicity for firm's pet charity (103 different appeals to the season); reading manuscripts. Signing my letters: Private Secretary—on one never to be forgotten and glorious occasion receiving a reply from the Minister of Guess What's secretary addressed to me: Dear Private Secretary, and signed Private Secretary; deep baying to deep, private secretaries on the line. 'The Minister hopes . . .' 'Would you be so kind as to inform the Minister?' 'Sir Phoebus hopes . . .' Ministerial and baronetly hopes, reliant upon private secretariat. Signing my letters: Charity Publicity. Signing my letters: Reader, for Editorial Manager. Signing my letters: Phoebus Ullwater *tout court*, without the hedging chivvying invaliant p.p. Phoebus Ullwater, in slanting ruffling swashbuckling forgery. Forgery.

I love Sir Phoebus, at this moment, I love him with a deep and grateful love. He is the only man with whom I have consistently (I think, perhaps he does not) behaved myself, as an efficient worker, as a willing donkey, as a happy equable creature, blandly and happily performing its duties; an *animula, vagula, blandula* of the office. So grateful to him that for him at least I can be no tearing devil sobbing and fighting. I look at him with a smiling, happy, guiltless face. I look at him across the desk. I laugh, there are always so many things to laugh about, and so much work to do. And the people who come in to see Sir Phoebus, all the Old Friends, they are all something to laugh at for me, they are all old jokes that never pall. And: How are you? How is Sir Phoebus?

Old Jew Topheim: 'Ah Miss Casmilus . . . Sir Phoebus, he is so charming, so tactful, so young. I saw him at the Duke's.' Topheim coughs modestly and swells visibly. He is genuinely attached to Sir Phoebus: 'Miss Casmilus I am devoted to Sir Phoebus Ullwater . . . *devoted.*'

I admire and like this Topheim, very wily tenacious and *fidèle* is this combative noble animal.

But this occasion *At The Duke's*. It is true that good-for-old Topheim got asked down to see P. on urgent matters. He came upon the boy, the sweet boy playing cricket. I gather this at least from his at first startling description: 'Sir Phoebus looked lovely in white.' What vision of shy girl, Greuze-girl, eyes downcast, prayer-book in hand, tripping devoutly to first communion.

But no, no. This is Sir Phoebus resplendent in cricketing. Sir Phoebus 'looking lovely in white'. The Academy Picture of the Year. The Bright White Flower of the Month of June, the Choice of the British Horticultural Society, the Choice of Society's Mamas of long years since. But now and ever, for one proud associate, *'looking lovely in white'*.

Dark bright face of Sir Phoebus across the desk, with perhaps misfortunes of his own heaping upon him, and no luck, no satisfaction, no revenge. How can I face that face, no longer myself the limpid *animula*, no longer *vagula, blandula,* no longer *hospes comesque corporis*. But scattered, torn, shattered; born for this only, for this present disarray; through long first centuries accrued, through fire, through ice, through tropic mud and ice again, the sorrows of Pompey, the troubles of Mrs. Haliburton, the unappeasable never to be appeased hunger of the ravishing Kismet, the Cornish diabetic, for ever eating and never nourished, never comfortable.

Oh uncomfortable Kismet, what troubles of yours compare with mine? Oh cat on cradle, oh baby adventurer betwixt cat and flood. Oh flood of tears' flow. Oh sweetest scent of death. Oh disarray, dismay, and dudgeon. Oh *comble* of her dreams, her dreams' worst devising. Oh too prophetic dream. Oh night of Pompey.

My sweet boy Freddy has left me.

No longer prancing forth light and malicious as tiger on padded paw, to play, scratch, pat, prod, prink; to hug, kiss, lick, bite; to lie in the firelight; to be happy; a hearth-rug's ivory tower of bliss, a little space, a time-pocket for love and play and friendship; long days in the summer, playing, tearing, laughing. Long happy hours sped. O'er-toppled towers of several ivories. Oh blessed tense that was not was.

For two years now has Freddy been my own peculiar friend and playmate. But now he is proud, revengeful; will have marriage now or nothing; will not have marriage now, for he is in a huff, a puff of huff I thought that should disperse. But now it will not. Oh Freddy, my sweet idiot boy, how can you be withdrawn so cold, so permanently huffish? You that had a loving giving face, a loving and inquiring charm, how changed you are, how different, how distant cold and dippy. How delicate was our relationship, how light as gossamer how strong as steel.

In the car again I say to William: How can we marry, how can we? Would it not be utterly foolish, utterly suicidal? He so poor, and I so poor, in this world's goods, in health, in strength of nerve and body? But was it for this reason so incumbent upon him, upon my lost fond Freddy to break and tear away the tie between us, formed unknown, unguessed by me, to tear the flesh away and bleed and bleed? *Die Liebe ist tausendform.* How impious to destroy because not usual.

My Freddy boy had many funny ways. Often he was saying things, you would say they were harmless things for a sweetie-pie that was so sweet to say. But no no, in the heart of the proud and satanic Pompey is such a white flame of antagonism that no, there was no longer any sweetie-pie, but a monster that was turning all the time and lusting after the habits and thoughts of the insignificant, the timid, the mediocre.

And so I was crying out: Oh Freddy forget your circumstance, do not be subservient to this circumstance. Soar up with me. Forget the Job-Job-Job, with all its paraphernalia of subordination, turning always upon the pivot of littleness, tunnelling, burrowing back, down and through, to something receding, ever diminishing, suffocating, close-cramping. Oh womb of that desire, of dark place of craven shielding. Peel off my wings and pare my claws. Steal dark dream of pride, nobility and death. Put back, pull down, clasp, cramp, imprison. *Oh, no, but love me, give me leave to soar. You shall be free, he said, I will withdraw.*

Did you know, Reader, that in the suburbs people are extremely class-conscious? I will tell you, forgetting myself to enlighten you. You must know that living with my proud kind aunt, my Lion of Hull, we have formed, the two of us, with my dear sister Mary on her returns from Ipswich, a duo-trio of non-communication. Often have I felt sad to see so many people about the streets of Bottle Green, and not to know at all who they are, or what they are doing or where they are going, or what they are thinking, or why. My life and soul and spirit go out to my darling friends who live scattered in town or in country. They must be exhaustingly visited, or like my darling Harriet exhaustingly accompanied to brasserie, bar, club, and pub. And this is why I am always looking so thin and rampant. I love them so much. Must see them. Must travel the long distance to or with them. But at home where I live there is no one I know except the lion my aunt. In town it is almost too exhausting, at home almost too quiet and isolated.

Oh now I am back in the car again, telling William, listening to William, quite unable to tell William, so profoundly disturbed, so dark, so very dark and *grimmig*.

I am in a sad autumn countryside. It is raining. The trees hang down, the trees' branches are so sad, they droop. And also now it is night. And I am passing alone, I am walking alone through the night. There is a country lane, but there are also houses, a few houses standing back from this country lane.

All the houses have bright curtains. The light is shining through. But outside it is not being so warm, so close, so womblandish as all that, it is cold and it is raining. There is a park lying behind high iron palings and the gateposts are like totem poles, like tribal deities. There is very much of Sir James George Fraser in those gateposts. I am thinking there is a great deal of Sir J. G. Fraser there. And now in imagination I am in the park. I am no longer outside of these gateposts, but alone within. The rain has stopped raining, and the moon has come out. It is silvering the rain-soaked, night-drooping sad-so-sad trees. And I walk towards the broad lake in Scapelands Park, the lake that I said, so many words, so many words ago. But the lake is unfamiliar. By night it is being rather hostile. And so cold I shiver, it is so cold. But even so I will not, I will never be so *womblandisch,* I will never give this all and everything up. Nor is it at all necessary for one moment, for one moment necessary at all. *Die Liebe ist tausendform.*

And you my darling Freddy, my darling little child, my dippy Freddy, affronted, disgusted, outraged and reproachful, *je me demande pourquoi.* There was never anyone as I who asked so much of nothing. Oh come on my darling Freddy and do not be so dippy.

Oh William, now you are telling me about Fanto. And this saves me again, and brings me back alive in time for that dreadful night park, that so dreadful place where all the time I am so distraught, I am so remembering and thinking back, very full indeed of remorse and disturbance. Ah distracting thought that creeps through and disintegrating mind, unwelcome worm. How stand up whole any longer against the treachery of thought acting upon weakness and despair.

Now William, rounding a corner of leafless Lincs, by a miracle escaping the ditch, is telling me about Fanto. 'How,' from the depths of my night of foreboding, 'how, William is Fanto?'

Fanto is the son, there is one son and three daughters, of a mismarriage. His father is the son of the Duke of Pena-Kolberg, that loveable and eccentric Italian whose life history is the subject of Hector Boltesta's perhaps most charming memoir. The old Duke died of snake-bite and a broken heart in 1901, the broken heart was because of this only son of his who, sent into England to study democratic customs, must go marry a peasant woman, no, it is wrong, in England it is a country woman. So. He was cut off, cast out, condemned. The name is Fantaccino now. The Pena-Kolbergs are but a memory, a Hector Boltesta memoir.

So one day William said: Come for the weekend. Mrs. Fantaccino will put you up.

So I came to stay with this English peasant woman. She had a very nice clean house not far from the sea. She was all the time rather worrying about her nice house, rather conscious of it, as if it were an honour hardly to be borne to live to serve such a fine house as that was. So there was in my bedroom a very grand looking piece of furniture. And I was wondering what this grand looking piece of furniture could be. Because in all my travels and goings and comings I had never seen such.

I have travelled and come and gone a great deal, I am a *toute entière* visitor. That is what I am being all the time. I visit and visit and visit, my darling friends, my less darling friends, my acquaintances. I am very grateful to them all. In visiting I find a very great deal of comfort and satisfaction, and each least place where I visit I am so enchanted and so happy that it is another visit, and that at the end of the time I may say: Good-bye and thank you, good-bye. And perhaps as I have said they will stand and smile, and say: Good-bye Pompey, come again soon. That is the very highest pleasure to me, that it is a visit that comes to an end, that may recur, that may again come to an end and be renewed. The rhythm of visiting is in my blood. Under what tutelary deity shall I place myself? Under Mercury, double-facing, looking two ways, lord of the underworld, riding on the white horse, riding through hell, opener of doors; Hermes.

Now this piece of grand looking furniture I am telling you about, it turned out to be a *commode*, that I had never seen before. So I began to think there must be something un-English too about this wife of the son of the great Duke, because surely English cottages do not have this grand and insanitary idea at all. *Où sont les commodes d'antan?* They are dead and buried with Celia and her morbidly body-conscious, body-hating Swift.

In the morning Mrs. Fantaccino brought me up my breakfast on a tray. I sat up in bed and pulled back the curtains. The room looked on to a long garden stretching down to a roadway that had now and then trucks and lorries passing along it, and the garden stretched down for 150 yards before you could get at the road. 'But oh,' said Mrs. Fantaccino, 'be careful, they will see you sitting up in bed.'

How the dwellers within and behind those curtains, shrouding the daylight or lit from within, how they are always so afraid of 'them'. Pull the curtains, bolt the door, lock windows, 'fast bind, fast find'. How they are crouching within and behind. Are they afraid of the homelessness of the wide universe? Are they putting this little shield of plaited light and warmth and littleness between them and the cold wide planetary spaces, that one day in life or in death they must tread alone?

The tall son of Mrs. Fantaccino has taken a wrong and a desperate turning in life, so William tells me, laughing and telling. I knew it. These children of the mismarriage they are all the time hating and fighting their peasant blood, and turning to the easy aristocratic ways of their father and their grandfather, the ambassador to the Court of Love and Beauty.

So. The son was a clerk in Whitehall, and the girls, two were in a hat shop and one was on the stage. So this is how it went. Fanto, the eldest child, was looking splendid, he was a splendid looking young man. But the canker was at his heart, eating it away. Oh money, oh bitter chagrin in the half-peasant half-seigniorial mind of wanting, wanting and never having.

So being so handsome, the old girls got hold of him. He went with the old women. They took him to dances and he danced them up and down, and they were looking rather fat and getting rather breathless. But dance she must, like the witch-woman in the story, *bis sie tot zur Erde fiel.*

But they never were *tot*. The vitality of the old girls, the awful energy of the after fifty, the undirected energy, again the canker eating away. So they must dance, febrile Old Girl dances with febrile young man. It is all so feverish and I think it has to be unhappy.

So eventually one Old Girl died and left Fanto money, mun-mun-glorious-mun. So off went Fanto and took a farm in Rhodesia, Rhodesia, fascinating country for the calm at heart, of mental and moral integrity, gall and wormwood to the distraught and febrile.

But oh alas the succeeding Old Girl had

her spider grip on Fanto and went *mit*. Never never could he throw her off and there was always more mun-mun-glorious-mun rolling in from this tenacious Old Girl friend of Fanto's.

Oh, he said, I wish the bitch goddess would die, oh how I wish her dead, 'would she were dead at my feet, and the share certificates and the bearer bonds and the cash at the bank and *toute la bagatelle* in her coffin'.

Unhappily rounding his bought acres, bought with the mun-mun-glorious-mun of the predeceasing Old Girl, all those acres shadowed by emptiness and black bile of the spirit, there he was, walking and wringing his hands: 'would God she were dead'; hate and exasperation rising in his heart and no satisfaction, no revenge. But what revenge, and for what, hopelessly in the toils, how could he sue for revenge? 'Why, even now,' said William laughing and telling, 'even now he spends no penny of his legacy. The new Old Girl Friend pays all. He does not even touch the interest.' So tied and taut and distraught and fainting and feverishly straining away, away he cannot get. So how is Fanto? That is how is Fanto. And the daughters have their own life *bei ihnen ist es ganz gleich*. And now, Pompey, how is Freddy?

Now you see it is quite simple, he throws the ball of narrative to me. Oh indeed how is Freddy? Oh how terribly tearing and distracting is this Freddy business. Now we are engaged to be married. That is a grand expression, we are engaged to be married, I have the *éclat* of the fiancée. But somehow marriage and being engaged to be married does not bite upon my consciousness at all, it is not right, perhaps it is not the right sort of acid, it has no bite. And so when we are engaged I move my mother's engagement ring that I had from her when she died when I was sixteen, this ring I shift to my engagement finger, it is like a game that has no significance but to play we are engaged. But it galls and wounds us this marriage game, and in our hearts we are beginning to think: Never never can we marry. And we are having no faith at all in this idea that should perhaps already a long time have been crystallized.

And I am now so full of pride and *désespoir,* like that great angel Lucifer that fell from heaven, over the battlements of heaven, and through space downwards to the heart of darkness. That was so fortunate in his lucy-falling star that had that great satanic Milton to catch him up where he fell. That great Milton that got shot up like me, *that with no middle flight*.

Ach Freddy, Freddy, *warum qualst Du nuch so?* How we have strained and strained against and away from each other, each trying to alter each, and so and so. And now I am remembering that I read in Blake's poems, I have read these very serious lines, very full of ominous portent are these lines:

Love seeketh only Self to please,
To bind another to its delight,
Joys in another's loss of ease,
And builds a Hell in Heaven's despite.

Oh now I am remembering these lines while I am talking to William, and remembering these lines and so full of bitterness and *désespoir* I feel at once that we are no longer engaged. And I take the ring and put it back on the insignificant finger, *Adieu, éclat de fiancée.*

Now I say. How difficult is life nowadays. But there must be freedom and generosity and truth and candour. There must be love and wisdom and honour. Nothing must prevent this, there would better be death. There is so much of this and that already between us, so much of You said, and I said, and You said, to be repeated with reproachfulness and no heat of temper but reiteration, You said, and so.

But if I said or you said, I have forgotten, at least I think it was not like that. It was not that way at all. The moment has flown from my memory, do not bring it back to trail its bright feathers in the mud.

And in this black minute of *désespoir*, I think, I think: Married to Freddy, in the high floating exaltation of these moments when imagination working on generosity all seemed so well between us, and all well lost for that life together, married to him in the morning, in the evening I should be dead. Dead and covered with shame and dishonour. *Je mourais ce matin digne d'être pleurée, J'ai suivi tes conseils, je meurs déshonorée.*

That is what poor wretched but simple and honourable Phèdre says to her ill-advising *confidante.*

How many ill-advising *confidantes* have not said to me: Marry, do not live alone. When you are old you will be sad, thinking you might have married, but now you are an old girl, unmarried, uncomforted, alone.

I tear into shreds these dishonourable *conseils.*

More closely they touched me who said: Marry now, quickly, while the flame burns. Do not wait.

William is counselling, warning: Do not marry, Pompey, do not.

Afterwards you will find it will be very desperately difficult very bitter indeed. But keep your high friendship and love, and leave marriage, leave it altogether alone.

But he is so sweet. He is my darling. He is my most darling Freddy. But look. He only did not understand. Is that a crime? That I should be so sad? And yet and yet 'I would rather be a king among mice' he has said to me.

And afterwards after this so famous marriage, shall I find the mind of Freddy turning inevitably *aux royaumes des aveugles* seeking safety in the mediocre and the insignificant?

Oh friends of friends, of this narrow-edged driving wedge that is driving between us. Oh how many words how many gestures.

'I like simple minds and kind hearts.' Ah now wait now just wait one moment, for I know these kind hearts and simple minds, they are not being so very kind and simple at all, they are often very narrow little minds that these people have, and they are not kind at all but very cruel very bitterly cruel, they are not growing at all but very entirely stunted. They turn away from the sunshine, they are strong to come together and in a mass of littleness to oppose every great idea that is at all difficult to understand, every great idea that is coming forth with blood and tears brought to birth they will beat it down and tread it down and tread it into the ground. Yes they will do this if they can they will do this.

Oh I know them very well they are as cruel as sin more cruel than death that great prince that must come up at the end. *Insuffisance,* defeatism and incorruptible fidelity to the worse and the lower, was ever a people that invited to look on this and on the other so unerringly chose the other? Apostles of the inferior, evangels of the All-Lowest, oh *royaume des aveules, je me demande pourquoi.*

It is I think that in these people, wronged insulted and rejected even in childhood there has grown up a desire for power and a self absorption a self-conceit turning mordant upon itself and in that self the seeds of intelligence uncared-for and neglected. Oh *männlicher protesting* mereness, oh inferiority lusting for power and by its own neglect of its own true happiness forced to live at what low level of intellect and spirit, taking pleasure in imagined insults and affronts, to brood upon them in the darkness and operating upon them to beget such knock-kneed down-at-heels wispish, waifish progeny.

Oh my darling Freddy do not be so deeply dippy. You have nothing to do with these people, nothing at all, they are not your people. Leave them to fume and brood and turn ever upon themselves, in what sad place of egotism and imagined injury, growing ever less, contracting, diminishing, becoming more apart and separate, dwindling, diminishing to death.

But in his extreme moods of exasperation he has said to me: Bring your ideas down to earth. You want sense knocked into you. Keep your feet on the ground. You want sense knocked into you. You should.

But now chaps is not this the very language of Mr. Mere that is so very mere like I was telling you that is Mr. Mere that would say to the Lord that Mr. Mere that would have said to the Lord that would have said: My dear Jesus Christ, my advice to you is bring your ideas down to earth don't, above all don't be hysterical. Keep your feet firmly on the ground. Plain ordinary men like you and me don't want to go gallivanting after these farfetched ideas. It's indigestion that's what it is. We all get these times now just the other day I was feeling mopish myself. Indigestion. I went to the chemists and got some of that Maclean's stomach powder. That put me right.

Oh Jesus Christ, in the mighty sweep of your divine mind, the sorrow of night space and the rushing air, the dark night and the soft plumage of the bird flying by night that brushes your exalted cheek, the wide and lofty thought sweeping ever upwards and outwards, bearing with it what agony of spirit and noble strife, this then is what this then is what.

Pompey was enamoured of a chimera. Hand in hand they ran through the deserted park land. It was night and a high moon sailed up above the treetops. Pompey and her chimera were in high fettle they laughed and raced there under the trees by the cold damp sand at the margin of the treacherous lake through the long swaying grass they fled chasing and beyond the boat house with the little boats lying upon their folded oars. There was a great space between the beech trees. There, under the full light of the hunter's moon, high riding in pride and integrity, Pompey's chimera seized her, and the *chimeraismus* departed, and there stood a little monster no bigger than her thumb, but she would not let him drum, and she fled, Pompey fled, and the high and mighty moon caught her up on its cold enchantment. She tore away the monster and left him with his feet firm upon the ground. But tearing away, she tore him too, and herself. And Venus, fast enemy to Artemis, and all the high cold emptiness which that night huntress chooses for her performance, Venus was very *farouche* and furious. Very *farouche* and furious indeed was Venus: Well, Miss, you've brought it upon yourself, and now you'll please to suffer for it. You can't go falling in love with a chimera just as you please, not just like that, not that way at all. Now you'll see, watch what I'll do to you, you proud prancing Pompey, you airy fairy piece of nonsense. You superior person, you *Hubris*.

And I remember again Phèdre and her: '*O haine de Vénus! O fatale colère! Dans quels égarements l'amour jeta ma mere!*'

Certainly *l'amour jeta* my mama in considerable *égarements,* though papa was hardly the monster for whom Pasiphae swarmed. And remembering my own mama's lesser *égarements,* I am thinking, now that the first pang of separation is over, and the moonlight of Diana's comfort strikes less cold, I am thinking that it is a very good thing that Freddy and I, by drift or delirium, did not get ourselves into the matrimonial swamp.

After my sweet boy Freddy, that is my

sweet boy Freddy left me, that is the sweet boy Freddy I was thinking, in my black satanic minute, was the sweet boy Freddy before he shed his chimera-ismus, I was very deeply and literarily sad. And at this time too, chaps, I had influenza. No Pompey, not influenza, yes chaps, influenza. And I was lying in bed, crying with influenza and exasperation, when into my bedroom came my Aunt the Lion of Hull. There was going to be a church bazaar. Auntie Lion was going to the bazaar as a fan. Now all the ladies of the parish were going to the bazaar as a fan. But Auntie Lion was not at one with her fan. Standing in front of the double mirror in the bedroom she was making lionish faces and noises because of the obstinacy of the fan: Now it is fixed how do I look?

So she was looking rather sweet but also so extremely funny I must not laugh. There was her face, and her eyes glaring like a lion that is furious in the jungle of the night, and her hair that has suffered so long the domination of the red hot curling tong, but has never for pride come to terms with that curling tong, this hair was rebelliously standing straight up on end, and round her head was a little piece of green baby ribbon, and at the back was this famous fan standing very stiffly on end, to keep in step with the bouncing front hair of my aunt. There were also three fans arranged spread-wise on each shoulder.

There was something of the fish about the

effect, a mighty fish, very deep and dark and dangerous, with the temperament of a lion, and the dirty old-fashioned look coming out of the eyes. But now it was all fixed and set in order. And so I could certainly say that it was looking very splendid, and it was the crystallization of a very unusual idea. This fish-fin-fan fair across in the church hall must have had a very frantic and esoteric appearance. But there is always to my mind something very frantic and esoteric about the old ladies of the parish, and their fairs, and all the time the swift current of their unguessable thoughts.

Darling Auntie Lion, I do so hope you will forgive what is written here. You are yourself like shining gold. When I think of what some women are like, I am full of humble gratitude and apprehension that I have you to live with.

And why apprehension? Because the Pompeys who are so clever to poke fun at the noble Lion, with his golden coat, his elegant tail, his neat shape, and the precise footfalling of his padded gait, have but themselves to thank if Lion in royal huff and puff, go move his house.

Now I must go back again and tell you about the way that letters are often being so very funny. When William was sick in hospital and making life a cruel and bitter burden for Miss Champagne that looked after him, when William was sitting up in bed, looking like George the Third, about this time when it was cold and dark and damp and February my darling mama died.

What can you do? You can do nothing but be there, and go on being there steadily and without a break until the end. There is nothing but that that you can do. My mother was dying, she had heart disease, she could not breathe, already there were the cylinders of oxygen. There was the nurse and the doctor coming day and night. But if you cannot breathe how can you breathe the oxygen? Even, how can the doctors help you. Or? You must suffer and then you must die. And for a week this last suffering leading to death continued. Oh how much better to die quickly. Oh then afterwards they say: Your mother died quickly. She did not suffer. You must remember to be thankful for that. But all the time you are remembering that she did suffer. Because if you cannot breathe you must suffer. And the last minute when you are dying, that may be a very long time indeed. But of course the doctors and the nurses have their feet very firmly upon the ground, and a minute to them is just sixty seconds' worth of distance run. So now it is all over, it is all over and she is dead. Yes it is all over, it is all over, it is.

Now William was a great friend of my mother's, and of my aunt's too. Though admiring her, and understanding all her lionish virtues, and her great strength of lion-heart and courage, and so, but he could not be so intimate with her to talk and talk and laugh and talk, the way he loved with my mother. And all his army friends used to throng our house, and listen and talk and laugh.

But there was one friend of his that was this *Tommy*, and Tommy had a great gift for letter writing, and he used to write to me a great deal when later on Tommy was sent to Wales. Though now I cannot remember what there was doing then on the Welsh front, but to Wales he went. And he used to write. And he would say, how beautiful the miners were looking, like children, so simple and strong. Because poor Tommy was neither simple nor strong. So it was a compensation for him, looking wispish and waifish in his khaki, to look at the miners, so strong and simple. And he said he felt so strongly about the miners he would like to kiss them.

Now here is a letter Tommy wrote me so many years ago from Wales. Here it is, word for word. I have kept it. I must hurry up to get it down. It is, I find it very sweet, and like Tommy, and funny.

'Dear Pompey, I send Knox's book at last with many apologies for delay. I hope you will find it acceptable. Ronny Knox is a saint and brilliant withal. I feel his weight on the side of orthodoxy very valuable. He is so intellectually sound. The book is charmingly written—his style is inimitable. I will send Rupert Brooke, also Maeterlinck, on too. I am suffering from flu and overwork. Kindest regards and much love from your sincere friend and admirer. Yours etc. Tommy.

PS. William has written announcing his intention of taking a regular commission. After the way he always slated the army and held it to ridicule-Well! In my church the Vicar has hung the flag of every nation because he believes in the catholic church embracing every nation. He's the limit. The colour of the central figure is gold. Our Lady's robe blue of course and St. John's brown. It is exquisite but the central figure is I consider out of proportion.'

This letter was accompanied by Ronald Knox's *Spiritual Aeneid*, and a postcard of the interior of the church belonging to the vicar *who was the limit*.

That letter with all its surge back to the war, and the first excitement and then tremendous importance of 'Ronnie's' conversion; or, as a strong minded church woman of my distant acquaintance said: 'perversion my dear, I always say—*perversion*' is very dim and dead now. But those times with their unquietness and bewilderment were very much alive and so now I have finished for ever with this memorial.

But why in pity's name, dear Pompey, do you write in here all this about the old letter you had from that Tommy-boy, that went away out of your life many, many years ago? And why so much about this William, and this other sad matter of the death of your mother?

Dear Reader, I will tell you the truth. It is indeed not a happy truth. There is at this moment a certain letter in my mind, a letter that I have received—not long ago, but now; not funny at all, but bitter; not from Tommy, but from Freddy. And just as I have forced my attention back to the funny letter I had from this Tommy, so I am forcing my attention away from Freddy to William, and forcibly-falsely saying: If Freddy is unkind, William must be kind, Freddy bad—*therefore* William good. But the sadness overlying it all is too strong, too strong. And this I have transferred to that older cause of sadness.

Oh beastly Mind, that is so strong to injure through deceiving, and wretched Reader, so mishandled and provoked.

Harriet has to know everything. She is so very happy for me that there is now this break in that impossible position between Freddy and myself. But I am not happy, not happy. My best friend Harriet you are a darling. How we do run round together. How very pleasant and easy and unexacting this friendship is, and how very unconsciously it goes very deep indeed.

Sometimes we are talking in brasseries, in bars, in restaurants, in Harriet's flat; we are talking easily and laughing a lot, about friends, about the office, about that funny Mr. Malaprop there is there. She tells me: He said: 'I took Mrs. So-and-So (his wife) to see So-and-So, but it was one of these sexy plays, we did not like it at all. Mrs. So-and-So did not like it at all. You know Miss Saye . . . my wife has no sex appeal.' Mr. Malaprop says 'summonsed' when he means summoned, and he always gets his wise-saws wrong. He says: the wish is farther from the thought, and he says: 'To be, or not to be—as they say.'

Harriet is also having troubles with her young man that sweet boy that is so very serious, and very teaching. Harriet is much more intelligent I think because she is not always being so serious. But this boy friend who is called Stephen, he is very serious indeed, and has never grown up out of being an undergraduate. He wishes to save the world. He has a very great deal to say about Major Douglas and Social Credit.

And Harriet is a darling and listens to him and comforts him for the sins of the whole world, which he must have upon his shoulders. But which were never meant for his shoulders at all. And he is suffering from this development-arrested-at-the-university. But Harriet is very adult, and is suffering from no arrestment in development. But has a quick bright flashing and illuminating mind. And sometimes when we are laughing together, and thinking that together it is easier and we have so very much more fun together than ever we do with our exacerbating, sulky messiah-maniacal, or cross-patchy young men, suddenly the talk will touch lightly on some subject and then up it flares, and out. And sweeping up and out, it is an exultation and an agony, but so sweet it should not be missed.

Harriet is not all neurotic. The verse she writes is very beautiful, calm. very classical and correct verse, very quiet indeed and beautiful. She has two books too in her mind she wishes to write. The one is about, it is about the history of fashion in its embracing all-embracing significance. That will certainly be a very comprehensive book. As Harriet says, the difficulty is where to stop casting one's net.

But with me, I shall have no such difficulty. I shall know when to stop, and I shall stop. And whatever I write then will be Volume Two.

But Harriet in her writing has a very exact and precise sense of form. And that is a thing I am not able to come by. Reader, it is a fault.

People have said to me: If you must write, remember to write the sort of book the plain man in the street will read. It may not be a best seller—but it should maintain a good circulation.

About this I pondered for a long time and became distraught. Because I can write only as I can write only, and Does the road wind uphill all the way? Yes, to the very end. But brace up, chaps, there's a 60,000 word limit.

Oh how irritated I am by this funny idea of keeping your feet on the ground. Spoken like an officer and a gentleman, Sir People. Spoken like a prig and a nincompoop.

It is very nice to have feet on the ground if you are a feet-on-the-ground person. I have nothing against feet-on-the-ground people at all. And it is very nice to have feet off the ground if you are a feet-off-the-ground person. I have nothing against feet-off-the-ground people. They are all aspects of the truth, or motes in the coloured rays that come from the coloured glass that stains the white radiance of eternity.

But I think it is very basely despicable to have feet on the ground and to want to have feet off the ground, and when you can't to say: Feet-off-the-ground person, so stuck up and superior, you wait till I get at you with a good dollop of nice black mud in your eye. Yah..

But now I think I must be fair to people. For I can understand how they are wishing to have their feet off the ground a little bit, and then being frightened and wondering if they can get back again to nice safe, warm, smelly earth.

And in Hertfordshire, where Freddy and I were running together for a long time, he has always been my sweet boy Freddy. And it comes back to me now when one evening it was getting dark, and I had walked myself to exhaustion, and to rest we were sitting in a graveyard, and it was raining. And these things make you realize how it is to be loved, and to sit on his knee in the churchyard in the rain, and how it is chimera-ismus may get set up and beginning its frantic course in the veins of two people who are unsuitably in love.

For in these moments of close approach and touch and unanimity, how easy it is to think no differences of mere thought can come between us. This is. And how sweet it was to see him at the barrier at the station when I was coming back from a visit, and to travel back with him to Bottle Green. And oh Bottle Green, as Hertfordshire has played its part. Bottle Green Bottle Green, Reader, have you ever seen Bottle Green?

Well then there is this suburb which is called like I said. I have never known anybody here except my Aunt the Lion, and I have wandered about having a *nostalgie* for this suburb but no means of getting into the inside-of it. And I have burned to know the suburb from top to bottom and round and about within. And Freddy has been my guide, my Virgil, in these regions. He has taken me in, I have visited in Bottle Green.

They are very kind and solid the people are, and they are very nice for a visit, say you come in from a walk and you are invited to tea. And there is a kind lady that is his mother. And there are scones for tea. And they draw up to the fire and there is talk about how awfully common the other people in Bottle Green are being all the time. And how they have their dinners in the kitchen, or sit in their shirt sleeves.

It is funny that all the time in suburbs people are being ashamed of being in suburbs, and are having to show that they are not like that themselves, not that way at all, you know. And there will be some courteous deprecating laughter.

And in this house of Freddy's they made me feel very welcome. And I could run into the kitchen, and could do everything but smack the dog, that was certainly needing to be smacked, because it was the sort of dog that will bark all the time, and jump up with his sharp claws out, that is death and despair to silk stockings or to loose woven woollen frocks.

And for this kindness, which I so much appreciated as a visitor, I am grateful to Freddy and to his mama. But I feel that I wish only to be a visitor, I cannot always be in that atmosphere, it is warm, but by and by it is too warm and too close. And if you are married it is very difficult to make it to remain always a visit.

But Freddy's heart is in these little homes. But to begin with I thought it was not. For to begin with he said many things that I thought he meant. That he said to say to please me. And so doing these things, and going places, and saying things to please me, I did not know it was for this. I thought it was because he thought it was. And oh how much trouble that has made between us. For always I took him at his word. And now that there is this break between us, he is saying: I did this to please you. And oh it has made a lot of trouble and wicked falseness between us.

And now that the bitterness of breaking has come I feel that he is so angry, and so resentful. And I dream that he is standing there with a white, sad, drawn and resentful face, and is misunderstanding how I am so sad, and is saying that I am a bloody highbrow, and is saying: 'Little pets like you, dear, must be lonely. You are only few, dear, must be lonely. If you do not like it, you can die. Well has not this always been your cry?'

But loneliness stays for a time, and he must know that too and be feeling that. And if I have torn him. And. I am then very sorry. And. The thoughts about the thoughts go round and round. But when the thousand and one hours are up, it will be over. So come thousand and one hours, more fleet-footed than you use, and cover it all over.

Now as to the second book that Harriet wished to write, that is about the sonnets. And laughing again she will say: It is about the sonnets. And oh how beautifully and loamishly sad are those sad and tearing sonnets, where everything is so unsuitable, and not on the ground at all. And all is being the expense of spirit in a waste of shame. But human beings must suffer, and must make suffering for themselves, and beat themselves up into spiritual frenzies, and oh death and desolation, and oh night space and horror, and oh keep my dream from me. And how very splendid it is that we can do all this to ourselves and have such a splendid and really ingenious gift for inflicting suffering upon ourselves. For suffering and strain are the gauge of life, and who wishes to live like a vegetable?

But sometimes suffering measures life and ends it. And then it is not so good at all. And between two people without knowing it a love may grow up, and a link may form, and no one knows or guesses. And so it has been. I did not know. But when it is over, it is over, then it is tearing inside, it is 'tearing in the belly' one would wish oneself dead and unborn. And one does little things and goes to see friends and does one's work and fusses with this and that and feels in one's heart the drift and dribble of penultimate things, and thinks: To-morrow I shall be dead.

And all the time it is nothing, really it is absolutely nothing, just an exasperation we have made for ourselves, an engine we have turned to slay ourselves. And we slay ourselves not for the person we love only, but for an end; or for a punishment for all that we have had to do in bringing it about. And there, chaps, lies the danger of accustoming oneself as a child to the thought of death by suicide. For if it is to pass, let it pass, only wait in silence and do nothing. But nothing is what I cannot do.

Oh quiet now Pompey, think of the little

birds. Have you ever thought of the birds? Do they fuss and fume for love? Oh look at that little bird sitting on the low bough swinging and singing to himself.

Now when I had flu, and sometime I must tell you about My Flu, I was lying in bed and looking out of my bedroom window, and they had taken down the curtain so that I could look out, and there framed in the window was our apple tree with birds sitting and swinging and chattering on every branch and twig. And it had been raining, and so as they sat and swung the drops fell down as clear as glass. And there was a hole in a roof over there and in that hole there was, I guess there was, a young family of birds and the father and mother were working hard digging worms and carrying to the young family that was inside. I used to like to lie and watch the birds. But they certainly were not so peaceful as a vegetable would be. But you cannot live like a vegetable. And as for the birds.

Last Saturday I met Harriet in town for lunch. First we were to meet at one restaurant but she was late. And it got hotter and hotter, and everybody was smoking, and everybody was. And so it was. Well. Harriet was half an hour late. So when she came I said: No, Harriet not here, it's too smoky too unbreathable. So we went on. And after we had found another restaurant and had lunch we said: What shall we do? So it was one of those hot hot days in November, when it is wet and hot. So we said we would go for a walk. So we walked up past Broadcasting House coming up from Piccadilly and into Regent's Park. And we walked beside the lake and stood for a time to watch the birds. And there they were swimming round on the brimming water, and there were swans and moorhens and seagulls and sparrows. And I thought: Keep calm Pompey, think of the little birds. And at that, up came a moorhen and bit a swan on the backside. The sparrows are so tame I accidentally ran into one a fat cock sparrow. I kicked it and stopped afterwards. It was not hurt. So walking and talking about Harriet's unusual Greek uncles, they are so unusual I cannot even begin to tell you, we came to a bus stop by Hanover Gate, and took a bus to Baker Street where we had tea.

Very dark and dashing was the afternoon sky beginning to be evening and night, and very high are the houses near Hanover Gate, they were marshalled rank on rank, and curtains drawn back from one wide window showed a child's nursery, the rocking horse, the books, the stuffed rabbit, the monkey, the bright coloured books. And above all the ferocious and resentful sky.

Oh Freddy, how keep you for ever at bay? The very words cry out to bring you back. Oh chaps he was sweet was Freddy, there were moods when never sweeter. But oh sweet of sweet, what helps, when sweet in but chimera-coat he trips beside? Now now that will do, do do. Let me have no more of that.

So. I went with a very special friend of mine that is called Topaz that I think I didn't mention before. Now I was certainly feeling sad, very sad and full of thoughts this night. But Topaz, God bless her heart, was in high fettle, having lacerated her soul, my dear chaps, to the uttermost marrow by stalking along the corridors of Broadcasting House, that house of. Well, Topaz said that Topaz felt, they didn't look the sort of young men there, they didn't look like they would be any menace to a girl that had been well brought up.

The castrating atmosphere of Broadcasting House is to my mind due to the air-conditioning. It fixes them, if I make my meaning clear, it prevents their getting *chimera-ismus*, and all the bells of hell go tingalingaling hang-over that way. Will you step up the apples and pears and have a cup of you and me? Freddy was a great boy for rhyming slang and taught me a lot that time we were in Cornwall that time I rode that high and hungry horse Kismet round the vegetable fields.

Well first Topaz and I went to a pub that's in St. Martin's Lane and had some on me. And she was telling me her marrow-harrowing experiences like I said. And I must say, and here never better, there's nothing like the bar if you're feeling a bit below par. So Pompey began to forget her sad sad love, that maybe never had a meaning, except in that ivory tower, that made such a good poem they all chose it first.

So presently Topaz and I got up and went across the road to that little restaurant that Harriet calls our thieves' kitchen, where for once they had something you could eat. So we ate and talked and Topaz said she guessed I had a *nostalgie* for Bottle Green. That is true. And that my hankering after my departed Freddy was certainly morbid. And I guess it is a deep-seated morbidity that I cannot out.

But I said how I wanted that bit about Bottle Green as well as all the pub-lub life in town. And how whenever a door had been opened, if it was shut, I could not help but cry and scream and tear and cry and weep and scream. Must that door be closed because we cannot marry, that never wanted to marry? And will the Kind Lady never receive again?

Well I was telling Topaz how now I was reading a fascinating play in German that is called *Der lebende Leichnam,* that is the living corpse by Tolstoi. It is done out of *russ* into *deutsch,* and it is certainly funny how the yeasty frothing Russian nonsense comes through the heavy precise German. It is very funny, very interesting indeed. But I never got to the end of this play yet, though I have read it many times and a very deep impression it has made on me.

And this play has the name *Manoli Privat* written on it in pencil. And now I cannot remember how that name came to be written there, but there it is, and not in my handwriting, but in a German handwriting. Now how would that be? I think perhaps Manoli Privat was an actress that played the Lisa part. Or may be it is a cigarette.

Lisa's husband Fedja has gone off to the gipsies. Where if you remember a long time back, I told you he found something that made him feel at home.

This poor Fedja, he was so much a Russian, that never did anything but talk and drink and feel he ought to be doing something else all the time a sad state to be in, he says: *'Ich suche nicht mich besser zu machen; ich bin ein Taugenichts; allein es gibt doch Dinge, die ich nicht ruhig tun könnte.'*

And the Prince Abreskoff that has come to the gipsies, has come to seek him out and bring him back, bring him back to his wife Lisa, that like me wants and does not want and tears and screams and *immer weint*, this Prince Abreskoff being a Russian is going to make the best of the country he is going over, he is not *just* going to bring Fedja back, no, he is going to satisfy his Russian-novelette soul, he is going to get to the soul of things—bottom of things to you common English.

So he says he says Prince Abreskoff, he says: 'My dear chap, how can you let yourself go to pieces like this?'—journey-backwards is the word, you might say go to pieces. And poor Fedja that is so unhappy, in the way that everybody is being so-o-o unhappy and torn to pieces, and having all the time a good cry, this poor Fedja can only think to say, he can only think to say he finds something among the gipsies that makes him feel at home.

I think I was too proud we must all have our womblands, mine is my ivory tower with Freddy open to the four winds of heaven, Fedja's is *'bei den Zigeunern'*. Freddy's is a little home. But oh it is only the words he uses that make me in my satanic mood, outcome of how many years of popular journalism, see instead of something you might like, just the something that is the something the advertisers are talking about, for their furniture, their radiogram, their famous washing-up machine, their house-mortgaging society.

So Prince Abreskoff says: *'Wie können Sie sich so hinreissen lassen?'*

Oh, my dear chap, that's easy enough, watch me. I can slip back, I can slip back through this crazy Russian-German play till I find what I am looking for.

Fedja is so tired, he is so absoutely tired out, he is so tired out and sick to death, to the point of death, all this agonizing and crying and self-laceration and pain, and oh woe woe to the House of Atreus. He is so weary in his soul he is now at last going to sleep, lulled by his own pet soma, which is the music, the wild and plaintive music of the gipsies. And he cries from his soul: *'Ach, wie gut. Nun nicht wieder erwachen . . . So sterben.'* And again later in this play a ripping, a simply ripping, chaps, piece of Old Russian Nonsense says: No but first I must tell you.

Oh, Pompey, now do sit down and tell us the whole story of this famous play from beginning to end. Now let us have no more, now begin at the beginning, and go on till you come to the end, please do, Gracious Miss.

No, then, I will not. Read the play for yourselves, besides I have never got to the end, and don't care, don't want to get to the end. I am *ungründlich.* Karl said so. Karl knows. Watch Karl.

So now. Fedja is concocting a famous plan, he is going to die, so that it can be, his death can be, a setting-free for Lisa and the simply *splendid* young man, chaps, that always wanted to marry her, before Fedja came along. But this other young man, that is Viktor Karenin, is so honourable, and his lady-mother is so high minded, and so sound orthodox, you know, that she cannot bear to see her son married off to a divorced woman, for did I say Fedja *willigt in die Scheidung ein.* That's *deutsch* for: he will divorce her.

But Karenin's mother is simply horrified by the idea. And here there is a perfectly priceless scene, chaps, between Frau Karenin and this Prince Abreskoff, that is always willing to be helpful to all his friends, and is always being *simply splendid*. That's two of them in one play, that makes poor Fedja look like two cents.

Now Prince Abreskoff is an old old soul-friend of Frau Karenin's. So she asks him to tea. And so in prances Prince A. and says: *'J'espère que je ne force pas la consigne.'*

That bit is in French because of the servants, and all the way through this scene they are suddenly speaking in this funny sort of stiff school-girl French, although the servant isn't there all the time. But perhaps it just helps them remember what old, old soul-friends they are.

So rather in a distraught manner Frau K. pours out the tea and says that Lisa has bewitched her dear son: *Il est ensorcelé, positivement ensorcelé,* if you please by this enchantress, you can hear Douglas Byng say it, can you not? who has made him so far forget his high-mindedness that he wants to marry *'eine geschiedene Frau'*—a divorced woman.

Then Frau Karenin, pouring herself out another cup of tea, can no longer hold herself in. And this, chaps, is what she says, and I will translate it for you afterwards, but you must have the German to give you the idea of how splendidly nonsensical it all is. So. *Ein gutes Weib könnte sich niemals dazu entschliessen, ihren Mann, einen guten Menschen,* (one up for Fedja) *zu verlassen. Ein sehr lieber Mensch.*

Aber wie er auch gewesen sein mag, quels que soient les torts qu'il a eu vis-à-vis d'elle—so darf man doch nicht seinen Gatten verlassen, sondern muss das Kreuz tragen. Ich versteh' nur eins nicht, wie Viktor mit seinen Anschauungen sich dazu entschliessen kann, eine geschiedene Frau zu heiraten. Wie oft hat er, und das ist nicht lange her, in meiner Gegenwart mit einem alten Freund unseres Hauses heiss darüber gestritten und ihm bewiesen, dass die Scheidung mit dem wahren Christentum nicht vereinbar sei, und jetzt mischt er sich selbst hinein. Si elle a pu le charmer à un tel point . . . Ich fürchte sie.

Now this is a genuine piece of old-time special pleading, when the tea cups are out, and the perfectly correct and always rather well-connected old soul friend is there. And the yellow silk curtains are drawn, and the fire is burning brightly, and the maidservant is hovering discreetly with the hot water, and then out goes the maidservant and they are left alone for this ever popular parlour game, this purely platonic masturbation *à deux*, this fascinating pastime that is so exquisitely and almost unbearably titillating—for those who like it, for those who like it.

Yes but what does it mean, Pompey, what is it all about? Well just quite roughly mind you, and no tying down word for word, the upshot is Frau K. says that no really nice woman could bring herself to leave her husband. And such a good man too and so nice. And even if he hadn't been, no matter, in fact so much better, there's a famous opportunity for the wife to get the *Opfer-slant* on life that is so good for the mortification of body, soul and spirit.

Masochism to you, friend, but *Opfer-slant* has a nice German-American sounding brass note to it, that goes well with this sort of talk.

Well to carry on from 'so much the better' which is where Frau K. stopped talking and Pompey took the line, she goes on to say, whatever of Mrs. Haliburton's troubles there may have been between them, One May Not leave one's husband, but rather One Must Bear One's Cross.

There you are you see, quite simple. If you cannot have your dear husband for a comfort and a delight, for a breadwinner and a cross patch, for a sofa, a chair or a hot-water bottle, one can use him as a Cross to be Borne.

It reminds me of our craft articles published, *passim,* in all our so-very-much-alike women's papers: How to make a knitting bag out of a top hat. May also be used for a beret or a tea cosy. Free patterns for all included.

I digress. Frau K. continues that, and it wasn't long since, and under my very nose, Viktor was saying that he did not think that divorce was compatible with the principles of Christianity. But then of course in *those* days. Well, that was before poor Fedja had gone off to find something to make him feel at home. And in those days Victor Karenin was wandering, not only in his mind as you might think, but actually in maiden meditation fancy free, having cast his eyes upon no woman and being as virgin as the north pole. Except of course for the one moment he was beginning to think about Lisa. But that was before Fedja's arrival, and never got any further and so doesn't count.

Can you not now begin to see how Fedja must have felt: I must get out of here? All this talk, and the *frou-frou* of women's petticoats, and the old soul-friends coming in to tea as the dusk was falling, and the talk and the talk and the talk going on all the time, and never arriving at any conclusion at all, and the hardly suppressed hysteria, and the longing, whimpering, whining, and wanting and not wanting?

Can you not sympathize how he might say: Oh to sleep, so to sleep, never to waken, and so to die.

But about this famous plan that Fedja began to concoct. How he would die and be done with it. And at the same time be noble in dying, and so leave a happy memory with his wife and her new husband, having by his death set them free to marry; and set Frau Karenin's heart at rest, since her frightful son would then be marrying not a divorced woman but a sorrowful widow. And Fedja would think how they—Viktor and Lisa—would talk together.

And he would here, he couldn't help it, being in a Russian play or novel you cannot help it, it must be. He would here give the knife a twist in the wound, imagining how they would say—and he knew what a smug-pug Viktor Karenin was, how they would say: '*My dear,* poor Fedja. Well we mustn't say anything about him now. After all, if he was a bit unsatisfactory at times, his death was *noble.* Now I don't often use a word like that, nor lightly, but when I say noble I mean . . .' and here Viktor would put his arms round Lisa, and pull her head down on to his shoulder, for a long, long kiss. And that kiss would have a very spiritual significance.

So poor Fedja was getting this plan together to die, and the fine piece of Old Russian Nonsense that was helping him was called Alexandroff. (I am very sorry, chaps, these Russian names are not very original. But there it is. This is Tolstoi and not the Ballet Club.) So Alexandroff, blowing off a bit to begin with on the subject of life and death, says: Don't imagine I'm going to try and hold you back. Life or death, it's all the same in the end for a man of genius.

Believe it or not, here's the German: *Leben oder Tod, das ist für eine Genie ganz ohne Unterschied.* Only Alexandroff just asks one favour, that, as a great personal favour, and I'd do the same for you, just as a great personal favour he asks that Fedja won't put the pistol to his head, not just at this particular moment, because 'the night is young'. What the piece of Old Russian Nonsense means is that he has still got a lot of Russian nonsense on the subject of life and death, a lot of this has to be worked off. It is all there, stuffed up with the bats in Alexandroff's head, just awaiting release.

So will the kind gentleman just order up another bottle of champagne, and listen. And listen. And listen. After all it's not asking much is it? And we have it on the best authority that the rest is silence.

Oh there is so much about it and about. How many words how many wretched words to be said, to be unsaid, to be said again, and gone over until you can no more. I can no more. Oh my darling Freddy I can no more. All I want now is like Fedja so to sleep and so to die. With your legal mind remembering and remembering so many things against me, so many things, so many charges that I cannot answer, cannot remember myself but know to be profoundly false, do you not think my darling that sometimes this lawyer's evidence you bring against me is of disservice to truth, and avoids the significant? There is for you a mass of detail and a false conclusion. For me but one significant fact that stands out, and for which I would live or die. But this fact. That is this fact. That is. That is what I cannot bring myself to write. It has been written so many times and soiled with every falseness and every base stupidity. Can you not see it?

Oh little creature form'd of joy and mirth,
Go, love without the help of anything on earth.

Indeed we have done this.

I have written that the thousand and one hours must pass, but for pain there is no measure of time. The nurses said my mother died quickly in a minute. But how long is that minute? and how long is this thousand and one hours, how long? You said that I should marry William. But that offends me more than anything you have ever said to me. For I am not at all in love with William, though I have a strong feeling for him, that grew up in those old days of the war, and is part of them, and of the death of my mother. But is not. Is not. Is not.

How profoundly impersonal is nature and how horrifying to the mind that is too little aloof, and yet upon no centre placed. To the heart of pain and the distraught mind, nature speaks only of death. Magnificent landscapes of the dream world, unfurling before the eye chasm upon chasm where no foot ever trod, and where the monstrous cliffs stretch down to an untouched sea, how often have I seen you from a distance and, drawn towards you, woken myself, to turn and dream again.

There was pity and incongruity in the death of the tigress Flo. Falling backwards into her pool at Whipsnade she lay there in a fit. The pool was drained and Flo, that mighty and unhappy creature, captured in what jungle darkness for what dishonourable destiny, was subjected to the indignity of artificial respiration. Yes, chaps, they worked Flo's legs backwards and forwards and sat on Flo's chest, and sooner them than me, you'll say, and sooner me than Flo, that couldn't understand and wasn't raised for these high jinks. Back came Flo's fled spirit and set her on uncertain pads. She looked, she lurched, and sensing some last, unnameable, not wholly apprehended, final outrage, she fell, she whimpered, clawed in vain, and died.